STRANGE GIFTS

STRANGE GIFTS

Eight Stories of Science Fiction

edited by
ROBERT SILVERBERG

THOMAS NELSON INC., PUBLISHERS
Nashville, Tennessee / New York, New York

 Published in Nashville, Tennessee, by Thomas Nelson Inc., Publishers, and simultaneously in Don Mills, Ontario, by Thomas Nelson & Sons (Canada) Limited. Manufactured in the United States of America.

ACKNOWLEDGMENTS

"THE GOLDEN MAN," *by Philip K. Dick.* Copyright 1954 by Quinn Publishing Co. Reprinted by permission of the author and his agents, Scott Meredith Literary Agency, Inc., 580 Fifth Avenue, New York, N.Y. 10036.

"DANGER–HUMAN!" *by Gordon R. Dickson.* Copyright © 1957 by Street & Smith Publications, Inc. Reprinted by permission of the author and his agent, Robert P. Mills, Ltd.

"ALL THE PEOPLE," *by R. A. Lafferty.* Copyright © 1961, 1972, by R. A. Lafferty. Reprinted by permission of the author and his agent, Virginia Kidd.

CONTENTS

STRANGE GIFTS

INTRODUCTION

Science fiction is, among many other things, a literature of wonders; and perhaps the chief wonder in our corner of the universe is the human mind. Through science fiction we can examine the full range of powers our minds encompass—including some powers not customarily included in our traditional five senses.

In an earlier anthology (*Mind to Mind*, Thomas Nelson, 1971) I offered a group of stories that explored one of the most frequently discussed of the extrasensory powers: telepathy, or direct communication between minds. The present book is in a sense a companion book, much more varied in its scope, that takes in other and less familiar aspects of the reach of the mind. I have tried, in making the selections for it, to avoid not only telepathy but also some of the other most familiar extrasensory gifts, clairvoyance and telekinesis and the other often-exploited science-fiction standbys. Instead, since the literature of wild-talent stories runs to thousands of titles, I've attempted to find ingenious and little-known stories about characters whose gifts are even farther out. Here we'll encounter a man who knows everyone in the world, one whose luck is always good, one who perceives color as odor and odor as texture, and many more. I think you'll find these strange gifts to be very strange indeed, and I hope you'll share my pleasure in this lively and inventive gathering of tales.

—Robert Silverberg

THE GOLDEN MAN

Philip K. Dick

This tense, swiftly moving story was written more than twenty years ago, at a time when it seemed that atomic war might well break out between the United States and the Soviet Union. Science-fiction writers then were much concerned with the possible genetic mutations of mankind that might emerge, induced by hard radiation, in the post-atomic-war world. Among the many writers to handle that theme was Philip K. Dick, then at the beginning of his brilliant career; and the ingenuity and narrative drive of such later Dick works as The Man in the High Castle *and* Do Androids Dream of Electric Sheep? *can readily be discerned in this supple portrayal of a unique superbeing.*

"Is it always hot like this?" the salesman demanded. He addressed everybody at the lunch counter and in the shabby booths against the wall. A middle-aged fat man with a good-natured smile, rumpled gray suit, sweat-stained white shirt, a drooping bow tie, and a panama hat.

"Only in the summer," the waitress answered.

None of the others stirred. The teen-age boy and girl in one of the booths, eyes fixed intently on each other. Two workmen, sleeves rolled up, arms dark and hairy, eating bean soup and rolls. A lean, weathered farmer. An elderly businessman in a blue serge suit, vest, and pocket watch. A dark, rat-faced cab driver drinking coffee. A tired woman who had come in to get off her feet and put down her bundles.

The salesman got out a package of cigarettes. He glanced curiously around the dingy café, lit up, leaned his arms on the counter, and said to the man next to him, "What's the name of this town?"

The man grunted. "Walnut Creek."

The salesman sipped at his Coke for a while, his cigarette held loosely between his plump white fingers. Presently he reached in his coat and brought out a leather wallet. For a long time he leafed thoughtfully through cards and papers, bits of notes, ticket stubs, endless odds and ends, soiled fragments—and finally a photograph.

He grinned at the photograph, and then began to chuckle, a low, moist rasp. "Look at this," he said to the man beside him.

The man went on reading his newspaper.

"Hey, look at this." The salesman nudged him with his elbow and pushed the photograph at him. "How's that strike you?"

Annoyed, the man glanced briefly at the photograph. It showed a nude woman, from the waist up. Perhaps thirty-five years old. Face turned away. Body white and flabby. With eight breasts.

"Ever seen anything like that?" the salesman chuckled, his little red eyes dancing. His face broke into lewd smiles and again he nudged the man.

"I've seen that before." Disgusted, the man resumed reading his newspaper.

The salesman noticed the lean old farmer was looking at the picture. He passed it genially over to him. "How's that strike you, Pop? Pretty good stuff, eh?"

The farmer examined the picture solemnly. He turned it over, studied the creased back, took a second look at the front, then tossed it to the salesman. It slid from the counter, turned over a couple of times, and fell to the floor face up.

The salesman picked it up and brushed it off. Carefully, almost tenderly, he restored it to his wallet. The waitress's eyes flickered as she caught a glimpse of it.

"Damn nice," the salesman observed, with a wink. "Wouldn't you say so?"

The waitress shrugged indifferently. "I don't know. I saw a lot of them around Denver. A whole colony."

"That's where this was taken. Denver DCA Camp."

"Any still alive?" the farmer asked.

The salesman laughed harshly. "You kidding?" He made a short, sharp swipe with his hand. "Not any more."

They were all listening. Even the high-school kids in the booth had stopped holding hands and were sitting up straight, eyes wide with fascination.

"Saw a funny kind down near San Diego," the farmer said. "Last year, sometime. Had wings like a bat. Skin, not feathers. Skin and bone wings."

The rat-eyed taxi driver chimed in. "That's nothing. There was a two-headed one in Detroit. I saw it on exhibit."

"Was it alive?" the waitress asked.

"No. They'd already euthed it."

"In sociology," the high-school boy spoke up, "we saw tapes of a whole lot of them. The winged kind from down south, the big-headed one they found in Germany, an awful-looking one with sort of cones, like an insect. And—"

"The worst of all," the elderly businessman stated, "are those English ones. That hid out in the coal mines. The ones they didn't find until last year." He shook his head. "Forty years, down there in the mines, breeding and developing. Almost a hundred of them. Survivors from a group that went underground during the war."

"They just found a new kind in Sweden," the waitress said. "I was reading about it. Controls minds at a distance, they said. Only a couple of them. The DCA got there plenty fast."

"That's a variation of the New Zealand type," one of the workmen said. "It reads minds."

"Reading and controlling are two different things," the businessman said. "When I hear something like that, I'm plenty glad there's the DCA."

"There was a type they found right after the war," the farmer said. "In Siberia. Had the ability to control objects. Psychokinetic ability. The Soviet DCA got it right away. Nobody remembers that any more."

"I remember that," the businessman said. "I was just a kid, then. I remember because that was the first deeve I ever heard of. My father called me into the living room and told me and my brothers and sisters. We were still rebuilding the house. That was in the days when the DCA inspected everyone and stamped their arms." He held up his thin, gnarled wrist. "I was stamped there, sixty years ago."

"Now they just have the birth inspection," the waitress said. She shivered. "There was one in San Francisco this month. First in over a year. They thought it was over, around here."

"It's been dwindling," the taxi driver said. "Frisco wasn't too bad hit. Not like some. Not like Detroit."

"They still get ten or fifteen a year in Detroit," the high-school boy said. "All around there. Lots of pools still left. People go into them, in spite of the robot signs."

"What kind was this one?" the salesman asked. "The one they found in San Francisco."

The waitress gestured. "Common type. The kind with no toes. Bent over. Big eyes."

"The nocturnal type," the salesman said.

"The mother had hid it. They say it was three years old. She got the doctor to forget the DCA chit. Old friend of the family."

The salesman had finished his Coke. He sat playing idly with his cigarette, listening to the hum of talk he had set into motion. The high-school boy was leaning excitedly toward the girl across from him, impressing her with his fund of knowledge. The lean farmer and the businessman were huddled together, remembering the old days, the last years of the war, before the first Ten-Year Reconstruction Plan. The taxi driver and the two workmen were swapping yarns about their own experiences.

The salesman caught the waitress's attention. "I guess," he said thoughtfully, "that one in Frisco caused quite a stir. Something like that happening so close."

"Yeah," the waitress murmured.

"This side of the bay wasn't really hit," the salesman continued. "You never get any of them over here."

"No." The waitress moved abruptly. "None in this area. Ever." She scooped up dirty dishes from the counter and headed toward the back.

"Never?" the salesman asked, surprised. "You've never had any deeves on this side of the bay?"

"No. None." She disappeared into the back, where the fry cook stood by his burners, white apron and tattooed wrists. Her voice was a little too loud, a little too harsh and strained. It made the farmer pause suddenly and glance up.

Silence dropped like a curtain. All sound cut off instantly. They were all gazing down at their food, suddenly tense and ominous.

"None around here," the taxi driver said, loudly and clearly, to no one in particular. "None ever."

"Sure," the salesman agreed genially. "I was only—"

"Make sure you get that straight," one of the workmen said.

The salesman blinked. "Sure, buddy. Sure." He fumbled nervously in his pocket. A quarter and a dime jangled to the floor and he hurriedly scooped them up. "No offense."

For a moment there was silence. Then the high-school boy spoke up, aware for the first time that nobody was saying anything. "I heard something," he began eagerly, voice full of importance. "Somebody said they saw something up by the Johnson farm that looked like it was one of those—"

"*Shut up,*" the businessman said, without turning his head.

Scarlet-faced, the boy sagged in his seat. His voice wavered and broke off. He peered hastily down at his hands and swallowed unhappily.

The salesman paid the waitress for his Coke. "What's the quickest road to Frisco?" he began. But the waitress had already turned her back.

The people at the counter were immersed in their food. None of them looked up. They ate in frozen silence. Hostile, unfriendly faces, intent on their food.

The salesman picked up his bulging briefcase, pushed open the screen door, and stepped out into the blazing sunlight. He moved toward his battered 1978 Buick, parked a few meters up. A blue-shirted traffic cop was standing in the shade of an awning, talking languidly to a young woman in a yellow silk dress that clung moistly to her slim body.

The salesman paused a moment before he got into his car. He waved his hand and hailed the policeman. "Say, you know this town pretty good?"

The policeman eyed the salesman's rumpled gray suit, bow tie, his sweat-stained shirt. The out-of-state license. "What do you want?"

"I'm looking for the Johnson farm," the salesman said. "Here to see him about some litigation." He moved toward the policeman, a small white card between his fingers. "I'm his attorney—from the New York Guild. Can you tell me how to get out there? I haven't been through here in a couple of years."

Nat Johnson gazed up at the noonday sun and saw that it was good. He sat sprawled out on the bottom step of the porch, a pipe between his yellowed teeth, a lithe, wiry man in red-checkered shirt and canvas jeans, powerful hands, iron-gray hair that was still thick despite sixty-five years of active life.

He was watching the children play. Jean rushed laughing in front of him, bosom heaving under her sweat shirt, black hair streaming behind her. She was sixteen, bright-eyed, legs strong and straight, slim young body bent slightly forward with the weight of the two horseshoes. After her scampered Dave, fourteen, white teeth and black hair, a handsome boy, a son to be proud of. Dave caught up with his sister, passed her, and reached the far peg. He stood waiting, legs apart, hands on his hips, his two horseshoes gripped easily. Gasping, Jean hurried toward him.

"Go ahead!" Dave shouted. "You shoot first. I'm waiting for you."

"So you can knock them away?"

"So I can knock them closer."

Jean tossed down one horseshoe and gripped the other with both hands, eyes on the distant peg. Her lithe body bent, one leg slid back, her spine arched. She took careful aim, closed one eye, and then expertly tossed the shoe. With a clang the shoe struck the distant peg, circled briefly around it, then bounced off again and rolled to one side. A cloud of dust rolled up.

"Not bad," Nat Johnson admitted, from his step. "Too hard, though. Take it easy." His chest swelled with pride as the girl's glistening, healthy body took aim and again threw. Two powerful, handsome children, almost ripe, on the verge of adulthood. Playing together in the hot sun.

And there was Cris.

Cris stood by the porch, arms folded. He wasn't playing. He was watching. He had stood there since Dave and Jean had begun playing, the same half-intent, half-remote expression on his finely cut face. As if he were seeing past them, beyond the two of them. Beyond the field, the barn, the creek bed, the rows of cedars.

"Come on, Cris!" Jean called, as she and Dave moved across the field to collect their horseshoes. "Don't you want to play?"

No, Cris didn't want to play. He never played. He was off in a world of his own, a world into which none of them could come. He never joined in anything, games or chores or family activities. He was by himself always. Remote, detached, aloof. Seeing past everyone and everything—that is, until all at once something clicked and he momentarily rephased, reentered their world briefly.

Nat Johnson reached out and knocked his pipe against the step. He refilled it from his leather tobacco pouch, his eyes on his eldest son. Cris was now moving into life. Heading out onto the field. He walked slowly, arms folded calmly, as if he had for the moment descended from his own world into theirs. Jean didn't see him; she had turned her back and was getting ready to pitch.

"Hey," Dave said, startled. "Here's Cris."

Cris reached his sister, stopped, and held out his hand. A great dignified figure, calm and impassive. Uncertainly, Jean gave him one of the horseshoes. "You want this? You want to play?"

Cris said nothing. He bent slightly, a supple arc of his incredibly graceful body, then moved his arm in a blur of speed. The shoe sailed, struck the far peg, and dizzily spun around it. Ringer.

The corners of Dave's mouth turned down. "What a lousy darn thing."

"Cris," Jean reproved, "you don't play fair."

No, Cris didn't play fair. He had watched half an hour—then come out and thrown once. One perfect toss, one dead ringer.

"He never makes a mistake," Dave complained.

Cris stood, face blank. A golden statue in the midday sun. Golden hair, skin, a light down of gold fuzz on his bare arms and legs—

Abruptly he stiffened. Nat sat up, startled. "What is it?" he barked.

Cris turned in a quick circle, magnificent body alert. "Cris!" Jean demanded. "What—"

Cris shot forward. Like a released energy beam he bounded across the field, over the fence, into the barn and out the other side. His flying figure seemed to skim over the dry grass as he descended into the barren creek bed, between the cedars. A momentary flash of gold—and he was gone. Vanished. There was no sound. No motion. He had utterly melted into the scenery.

"What was it this time?" Jean asked wearily. She came over to her father and threw herself down in the shade. Sweat glowed on her smooth neck and upper lip; her sweat shirt was streaked and damp. "What did he see?"

"He was after something," Dave stated, coming up.

Nat grunted. "Maybe. There's no telling."

"I guess I better tell Mom not to set a place for him," Jean said. "He probably won't be back."

Anger and futility descended over Nat Johnson. No, he wouldn't be back. Not for dinner and probably not the next day—or the one after that. He'd be gone God only knew how long. Or where. Or why. Off by himself, alone someplace. "If I thought there was any use," Nat began, "I'd send you two after him. But there's no—"

He broke off. A car was coming up the dirt road toward the farmhouse. A dusty, battered old Buick. Behind the wheel sat a plump, red-faced man in a gray suit, who waved cheerfully at them as the car sputtered to a stop and the motor died into silence.

"Afternoon," the man nodded, as he climbed out of the car. He tipped his hat pleasantly. He was middle-aged, genial-looking, perspiring freely as he crossed the dry ground toward the porch. "Maybe you folks can help me."

"What do you want?" Nat Johnson demanded hoarsely. He was frightened. He watched the creek bed out of the corner of his eye, praying silently. God, if only he *stayed* away. Jean was breathing quickly, sharp little gasps. She was terrified. Dave's face was expressionless, but all color had drained from it. "Who are you?" Nat demanded.

"Name's Baines. George Baines." The man held out his hand but Johnson ignored it. "Maybe you've heard of me. I own the Pacifica Development Corporation. We built all those little bomb-proof houses just outside town. Those little round ones you see as you come up the main highway from Lafayette."

"What do you want?" Johnson held his hands steady with an effort. He'd never heard of the man, although he'd noticed the housing tract. It couldn't be missed—a great ant heap of ugly pill-boxes straddling the highway. Baines looked like the kind of man who'd own them. But what did he want here?

"I've bought some land up this way," Baines was explaining. He rattled a sheaf of crisp papers. "This is the deed, but I'll be damned if I can find it." He grinned good-naturedly. "I know it's around this way, someplace, this side of the state road. According to the clerk at the County Recorder's Office, a mile or so this side of that hill over there. But I'm no damn good at reading maps."

"It isn't around here," Dave broke in. "There's only farms around here. Nothing for sale."

"This is a farm, son," Baines said genially. "I bought it for myself and my missus. So we could settle down." He wrinkled his pug nose. "Don't get the wrong idea—I'm not putting up any tracts around here. This is strictly for myself. An old farmhouse, twenty acres, a pump, and a few oak trees—"

"Let me see the deed." Johnson grabbed the sheaf of papers, and while Baines blinked in astonishment, he leafed rapidly through them. His face hardened and he handed them back. "What are you up to? This deed is for a parcel fifty miles from here."

"Fifty miles!" Baines was dumfounded. "No kidding? But the clerk told me—"

Johnson was on his feet. He towered over the fat man. He was in top-notch physical shape—and he was plenty damn suspicious. "Clerk, hell. You get back into your car and drive out of here. I don't know what you're after, or what you're here for, but I want you off my land."

In Johnson's massive fist something sparkled. A metal tube that gleamed ominously in the midday sunlight. Baines saw it—and gulped. "No offense, mister." He backed nervously away. "You folks sure are touchy. Take it easy, will you?"

Johnson said nothing. He gripped the lash-tube tighter and waited for the fat man to leave.

But Baines lingered. "Look, buddy. I've been driving around this furnace five hours, looking for my damn place. Any objection to my using your—facilities?"

Johnson eyed him with suspicion. Gradually the suspicion turned to disgust. He shrugged. "Dave, show him where the bathroom is."

"Thanks." Baines grinned thankfully. "And if it wouldn't be too much trouble, maybe a glass of water. I'd be glad to pay you for it." He chuckled knowingly. "Never let the city people get away with anything, eh?"

"Christ." Johnson turned away in revulsion as the fat man lumbered after his son, into the house.

"Dad," Jean whispered. As soon as Baines was inside she hurried up onto the porch, eyes wide with fear. "Dad, do you think he—"

Johnson put his arm around her. "Just hold on tight. He'll be gone, soon."

The girl's dark eyes flashed with mute terror. "Every time the man from the water company, or the tax collector, some tramp, children, *anybody* comes around, I get a terrible stab of pain—here." She clutched at her heart, hand against her breasts. "It's been that way eighteen years. How much longer can we keep it going? *How long?*"

The man named Baines emerged gratefully from the bathroom. Dave Johnson stood silently by the door, body rigid, youthful face stony.

"Thanks, son," Baines sighed. "Now where can I get a glass of cold water?" He smacked his thick lips in anticipation. "After you've been driving around the sticks looking for a dump some red-hot real estate agent stuck you with—"

Dave headed into the kitchen. "Mom, this man wants a drink of water. Dad said he could have it."

Dave had turned his back. Baines caught a brief glimpse of the mother, gray-haired, small, moving toward the sink with a glass, face withered and drawn, without expression.

Then Baines hurried from the room, down a hall. He passed through a bedroom, pulled a door open, found himself facing a closet. He turned and raced back, through the living room, into a dining room, then another bedroom. In a brief instant he had gone through the whole house.

He peered out a window. The back yard. Remains of a rusting truck. Entrance of an underground bomb shelter. Tin cans. Chickens scratching around. A dog, asleep under a shed. A couple of old auto tires.

He found a door leading out. Soundlessly, he tore the door open and stepped outside. No one was in sight. There was a barn, a leaning, ancient wood structure. Cedar trees beyond, a creek of some kind. What had once been an outhouse.

Baines moved cautiously around the side of the house. He had perhaps thirty seconds. He had left the door of the bathroom closed; the boy would think he had gone back in there. Baines looked into the house through a window. A large closet, filled with old clothing, boxes, and bundles of magazines.

He turned and started back. He reached the corner of the house and started around it.

Nat Johnson's gaunt shape loomed up and blocked his way. "All right, Baines. You asked for it."

A pink flash blossomed. It shut out the sunlight in a single blinding burst. Baines leaped back and clawed at his coat pocket. The edge of the flash caught him and he half fell, stunned by the force. His suit-shield sucked in the energy and discharged it, but the power rattled his teeth and for a moment he jerked like a puppet on a string. Darkness ebbed around him. He could feel the mesh of the shield glow white, as it absorbed the energy and fought to control it.

His own tube came out—and Johnson had no shield. "You're under arrest," Baines muttered grimly. "Put down your tube and your hands up. And call your family." He made a motion with the tube. "Come on, Johnson. Make it snappy."

The lash-tube wavered and then slipped from Johnson's fingers. "You're still alive." Dawning horror crept across his face. "Then you must be—"

Dave and Jean appeared. *"Dad!"*

"Come over here," Baines ordered. "Where's your mother?"

Dave jerked his head numbly. "Inside."

"Get her and bring her here."

"You're DCA," Nat Johnson whispered.

Baines didn't answer. He was doing something with his neck, pulling at the flabby flesh. The wiring of a contact mike glittered as he slipped it from a fold between two chins and into his pocket. From the dirt road came the sound of motors, sleek purrs that rapidly grew louder. Two teardrops of black metal came gliding up and parked beside the house. Men swarmed out, in the dark gray-green of the Government Civil Police. In the sky, swarms of black dots were descending, clouds of ugly flies that darkened the sun as they spilled out men and equipment. The men drifted slowly down.

"He's not here," Baines said, as the first man reached him. "He got away. Inform Wisdom back at the lab."

"We've got this section blocked off."

Baines turned to Nat Johnson, who stood in dazed silence, uncomprehending, his son and daughter beside him. "How did he know we were coming?" Baines demanded.

"I don't know," Johnson muttered. "He just—knew."

"A telepath?"

"I don't know."

Baines shrugged. "We'll know soon. A clamp is out, all around here. He can't get past, no matter what the hell he can do. Unless he can dematerialize himself."

"What'll you do with him when you—if you catch him?" Jean asked huskily.

"Study him."

"And then kill him?"

"That depends on the lab evaluation. If you could give me more to work on, I could predict better."

"We can't tell you anything. We don't know anything more." The girl's voice rose with desperation. "He doesn't talk."

Baines jumped. "*What?*"

"He doesn't talk. He never talked to us. Ever."

"How old is he?"

"Eighteen."

"No communication." Baines was sweating. "In eighteen years there hasn't been any semantic bridge between you? Does he have *any* contact? Signs? Codes?"

"He—ignores us. He eats here, stays with us. Sometimes he plays when we play. Or sits with us. He's gone days on end. We've never been able to find out what he's doing—or where. He sleeps in the barn—by himself."

"Is he really gold-colored?"

"Yes."

"Skin, as well as hair?"

"Skin, eyes, hair, nails. Everything."

"And he's large? Well formed?"

It was a moment before the girl answered. A strange emotion stirred her drawn features, a momentary glow. "He's incredibly beautiful. A god. A god come down to earth." Her lips twisted. "You won't find him. He can do things. Things you have no comprehension of. Powers so far beyond your limited—"

"You don't think we'll get him?" Baines frowned. "More teams are landing all the time. You've never seen an Agency clamp in operation. We've had sixty years to work out all the bugs. If he gets away it'll be the first time—"

Baines broke off abruptly. Three men were quickly approaching the porch. Two green-clad Civil Police. And a third man between them. A man who moved silently, lithely, a faintly luminous shape that towered above them.

"Cris!" Jean screamed.

"We got him," one of the police said.

Baines fingered his lash-tube uneasily. "Where? How?"

"He gave himself up," the policeman answered, voice full of awe. "He came to us voluntarily. Look at him. He's like a metal statue. Like some sort of—god."

The golden figure halted for a moment beside Jean. Then it turned slowly, calmly, to face Baines.

"Cris!" Jean shrieked. *"Why did you come back?"*

The same thought was eating at Baines, too. He shoved it aside —for the time being. "Is the jet out front?" he demanded quickly.

"Ready to go," one of the CP answered.

"Fine." Baines strode past them, down the steps and onto the dirt field. "Let's go. I want him taken directly to the lab." For a moment he studied the massive figure who stood calmly between the two Civil Policemen. Beside him, they seemed to have shrunk, become ungainly and repellent. Like dwarfs . . . What had Jean said? *A god come to earth.* Baines broke angrily away. "Come on," he muttered brusquely. "This one may be tough; we've never run up against one like it before. We don't know what the hell it can do."

The chamber was empty, except for the seated figure. Four bare walls, floor, and ceiling. A steady glare of white light relentlessly etched every corner of the chamber. Near the top of the far wall ran a narrow slot, the view windows through which the interior of the chamber was scanned.

The seated figure was quiet. He hadn't moved since the chamber locks had slid into place, since the heavy bolts had fallen from outside and the rows of bright-faced technicians had taken their places at the view windows. He gazed down at the floor, bent forward, hands clasped together, face calm, almost expressionless. In four hours he hadn't moved a muscle.

"Well?" Baines said. "What have you learned?"

Wisdom grunted sourly. "Not much. If we don't have him doped out in forty-eight hours we'll go ahead with the euth. We can't take any chances."

"You're thinking about the Tunis type," Baines said. He was, too. They had found ten of them, living in the ruins of the abandoned North African town. Their survival method was simple. They killed and absorbed other life forms, then imitated them and took their places. Chameleons, they were called. It had cost sixty lives before the last one was destroyed. Sixty top-level experts, highly trained DCA men.

"Any clues?" Baines asked.

"He's different as hell. This is going to be tough." Wisdom thumbed a pile of tape-spools. "This is the complete report, all the material we got from Johnson and his family. We pumped them with the psych-wash, then let them go home. Eighteen years—and no semantic bridge. Yet, he looks fully developed. Mature at thirteen—a shorter, faster life cycle than ours. But why the mane? All the gold fuzz? Like a Roman monument that's been gilded."

"Has the report come in from the analysis room? You had a wave-shot taken, of course."

"His brain pattern has been fully scanned. But it takes time for them to plot it out. We're all running around like lunatics while he just sits there!" Wisdom poked a stubby finger at the window. "We caught him easily enough. He can't have *much*, can he? But I'd like to know what it is. Before we euth him."

"Maybe we should keep him alive until we know."

"Euth in forty-eight hours," Wisdom repeated stubbornly. "Whether we know or not. I don't like him. He gives me the creeps."

Wisdom stood chewing nervously on his cigar, a red-haired, beefy-faced man, thick and heavy set, with a barrel chest and cold, shrewd eyes deep set in his hard face. Ed Wisdom was Director of DCA's North American Branch. But right now he was worried. His tiny eyes darted back and forth, alarmed flickers of gray in his brutal, massive face.

"You think," Baines said slowly, "this is *it?*"

"I always think so," Wisdom snapped. "I have to think so."

"I mean–"

"I know what you mean." Wisdom paced back and forth among the study tables, technicians at their benches, equipment and humming computers. Buzzing tape slots and research hook-ups. "This thing lived eighteen years with his family and *they* don't understand it. *They* don't know what it has. They know what it does, but not how."

"What does it do?"

"It knows things."

"What kind of things?"

Wisdom grabbed his lash-tube from his belt and tossed it on a table. "Here."

"What?"

"Here." Wisdom signaled, and a view window was slid back an inch. "Shoot him."

Baines blinked. "You said forty-eight hours."

With a curse, Wisdom snatched up the tube, aimed it through the window directly at the seated figure's back, and squeezed the trigger.

A blinding flash of pink. A cloud of energy blossomed in the center of the chamber. It sparkled, then died into dark ash.

"Good God!" Baines gasped. "You–"

He broke off. The figure was no longer sitting. As Wisdom fired, it had moved in a blur of speed, away from the blast, to the corner of the chamber. Now it was slowly coming back, face blank, still absorbed in thought.

"Fifth time," Wisdom said, as he put his tube away. "Last time Jamison and I fired together. Missed. He knew exactly when the bolts would hit. And where."

Baines and Wisdom looked at each other. Both of them were thinking the same thing. "But even reading minds wouldn't tell him where they were going to hit," Baines said. "When, maybe. But not where. Could you have called your own shots?"

"Not mine," Wisdom answered flatly. "I fired fast, damn near at random." He frowned. "*Random.* We'll have to make a test of this." He waved a group of technicians over. "Get a construction team up here. On the double." He grabbed paper and pen and began sketching.

While construction was going on, Baines met his fiancée in the lobby outside the lab, the great central lounge of the DCA Building.

"How's it coming?" she asked. Anita Ferris was tall and blond, with blue eyes and a mature, carefully cultivated figure. An attractive, competent-looking woman in her late twenties. She wore a metal-foil dress and cape—with a red-and-black stripe on the sleeve, the emblem of the A-Class. Anita was Director of the Semantics Agency, a top-level government coordinator. "Anything of interest, this time?"

"Plenty." Baines guided her from the lobby into the dim recess of the bar. Music played softly in the background, a shifting variety of patterns formed mathematically. Dim shapes moved expertly through the gloom, from table to table. Silent, efficient robot waiters.

As Anita sipped her Tom Collins, Baines outlined what they had found.

"What are the chances," Anita asked slowly, "that he's built up some kind of deflection cone? There was one kind that warped their environment by direct mental effort. No tools. Direct mind to matter."

"Psychokinetics?" Baines drummed restlessly on the table top. "I doubt it. The thing has ability to predict, not to control. He can't stop the beams, but he can sure as hell get out of the way."

"Does he jump between the molecules?"

Baines wasn't amused. "This is serious. We've handled these things sixty years—longer than you and I have been around added together. Eighty-seven types of deviants have shown up, real mutants that could reproduce themselves, not mere freaks. This is the eighty-eighth. We've been able to handle each of them in turn. But this—"

"Why are you so worried about this one?"

"First, it's eighteen years old. That in itself is incredible. Its family managed to hide it that long."

"Those women around Denver were older than that. Those ones with–"

"They were in a government camp. Somebody high up was toying with the idea of allowing them to breed. Some sort of industrial use. We withheld euth for years. But Cris Johnson stayed alive *outside our control.* Those things at Denver were under constant scrutiny."

"Maybe he's harmless. You always assume a deeve is a menace. He might even be beneficial. Somebody thought those women might work in. Maybe this thing has something that would advance the race."

"*Which* race? Not the human race. It's the old 'the operation was a success but the patient died' routine. If we introduce a mutant to keep us going it'll be mutants, not us, who'll inherit the earth. It'll be mutants surviving for their own sake. Don't think for a moment we can put padlocks on them and expect them to serve us. If they're really superior to Homo sapiens, they'll win out in even competition. To survive, we've got to cold-deck them right from the start."

"In other words, we'll know Homo superior when he comes–by definition. He'll be the one we won't be able to euth."

"That's about it," Baines answered. "Assuming there *is* a Homo superior. Maybe there's just Homo peculiar. Homo with an improved line."

"The Neanderthal probably thought the Cro-Magnon man had merely an improved line. A little more advanced ability to conjure up symbols and shape flint. From your description, this thing is more radical than a mere improvement."

"This thing," Baines said slowly, "has an ability to predict. So far, it's been able to stay alive. It's been able to cope with situations better than you or I could. How long do you think we'd stay alive in that chamber, with energy beams blazing down at us? In a sense it's got the ultimate survival ability. If it can always be accurate–"

A wall-speaker sounded. "Baines, you're wanted in the lab. Get the hell out of the bar and upramp."

Baines pushed back his chair and got to his feet. "Come along.

You may be interested in seeing what Wisdom has got dreamed up."

A tight group of top-level DCA officials stood around in a circle, middle-aged, gray-haired, listening to a skinny youth in a white shirt and rolled-up sleeves explaining an elaborate cube of metal and plastic that filled the center of the view platform. From it jutted an ugly array of tube snouts, gleaming muzzles that disappeared into an intricate maze of wiring.

"This," the youth was saying briskly, "is the first real test. It fires at random—as nearly random as we can make it, at least. Weighted balls are thrown up in an air stream, then dropped free to fall back and cut relays. They can fall in almost any pattern. The thing fires according to their pattern. Each drop produces a new configuration of timing and position. Ten tubes, in all. Each will be in constant motion."

"And *nobody* knows how they'll fire?" Anita asked.

"Nobody." Wisdom rubbed his thick hands together. "Mind reading won't help him, not with this thing."

Anita moved over to the view windows, as the cube was rolled into place. She gasped. "Is that him?"

"What's wrong?" Baines asked.

Anita's cheeks were flushed. "Why, I expected a—a *thing*. My God, he's beautiful! Like a golden statue. Like a deity!"

Baines laughed. "He's eighteen years old, Anita. Too young for you."

The woman was still peering through the view window. "Look at him. Eighteen? I don't believe it."

Cris Johnson sat in the center of the chamber, on the floor. A posture of contemplation, head bowed, arms folded, legs tucked under him. In the stark glare of the overhead lights his powerful body glowed and rippled, a shimmering figure of downy gold.

"Pretty, isn't he?" Wisdom muttered. "All right. Start it going."

"You're going to *kill* him?" Anita demanded.

"We're going to try."

"But he's—" She broke off uncertainly. "He's not a monster. He's not like those others, those hideous things with two heads, or those insects. Or those awful things from Tunis."

"What is he, then?" Baines asked.

"I don't know. But you can't just *kill* him. It's terrible!"

The cube clicked into life. The muzzles jerked, silently altered position. Three retracted, disappeared into the body of the cube. Others came out. Quickly, efficiently, they moved into position—and abruptly, without warning, opened fire.

A staggering burst of energy fanned out, a complex pattern that altered each moment, different angles, different velocities, a bewildering blur that cracked from the windows down into the chamber.

The golden figure moved. He dodged back and forth, expertly avoiding the bursts of energy that seared around him on all sides. Rolling clouds of ash obscured him; he was lost in a mist of crackling fire and ash.

"Stop it!" Anita shouted. "For God's sake, you'll destroy him!"

The chamber was an inferno of energy. The figure had completely disappeared. Wisdom waited a moment, then nodded to the technicians operating the cube. They touched guide buttons and the muzzles slowed and died. Some sank back into the cube. All became silent. The works of the cube ceased humming.

Cris Johnson was still alive. He emerged from the settling clouds of ash, blackened and singed. But unhurt. He had avoided each beam. He had weaved between them and among them as they came, a dancer leaping over glittering sword-points of pink fire. He had survived.

"No," Wisdom murmured, shaken and grim. "Not a telepath. Those were at random. No prearranged pattern."

The three of them looked at each other, dazed and frightened. Anita was trembling. Her face was pale and her blue eyes were wide. "What, then?" she whispered. "What is it? What does he have?"

"He's a good guesser," Wisdom suggested.

"He's not guessing," Baines answered. "Don't kid yourself. That's the whole point."

"No, he's not guessing." Wisdom nodded slowly. "He *knew*. He predicted each strike. I wonder. . . . *Can* he err? *Can* he make a mistake?"

"We caught him," Baines pointed out.

"You said he came back voluntarily." There was a strange look on Wisdom's face. "Did he come back *after* the clamp was up?"

Baines jumped. "Yes, after."

"He couldn't have got through the clamp. So he came back." Wisdom grinned wryly. "The clamp must actually have been perfect. It was supposed to be."

"If there had been a single hole," Baines murmured, "he would have known it—gone through."

Wisdom ordered a group of armed guards over. "Get him out of there. To the euth stage."

Anita shrieked. "Wisdom, you can't—"

"He's too far ahead of us. We can't compete with him." Wisdom's eyes were bleak. "We can only guess what's going to happen. He *knows*. For him, it's a sure thing. I don't think it'll help him at euth, though. The whole stage is flooded simultaneously. Instantaneous gas, released throughout." He signaled impatiently to the guards. "Get going. Take him down right away. Don't waste any time."

"Can we?" Baines murmured thoughtfully.

The guards took up positions by one of the chamber locks. Cautiously, the tower control slid the lock back. The first two guards stepped cautiously in, lash-tubes ready.

Cris stood in the center of the chamber. His back was to them as they crept toward him. For a moment he was silent, utterly unmoving. The guards fanned out, as more of them entered the chamber. Then—

Anita screamed. Wisdom cursed. The golden figure spun and leaped forward, in a flashing blur of speed. Past the triple line of guards, through the lock and into the corridor.

"Get him!" Baines shouted.

Guards milled everywhere. Flashes of energy lit up the corridor, as the figure raced among them, up the ramp.

"No use," Wisdom said calmly. "We can't hit him." He touched a button, then another. "But maybe this will help."

"What—" Baines began. But the leaping figure shot abruptly at him, and he dropped to one side. The figure flashed past. It ran effortlessly, face without expression, dodging and jumping as the energy beams seared around it.

For an instant the golden face loomed up before Baines. It passed and disappeared down a side corridor. Guards rushed after it, kneeling and firing, shouting orders excitedly. In the bowels of the building, heavy guns were rumbling up. Locks slid into place as escape corridors were systematically sealed off.

"Good God," Baines gasped, as he got to his feet. "Can't he do anything but run?"

"I gave orders," Wisdom said, "to have the building isolated. There's no way out. Nobody comes and nobody goes. He's loose here in the building—but he won't get out."

"If there's one exit overlooked, he'll know it," Anita pointed out shakily.

"We won't overlook any exit. We got him once; we'll get him again."

A messenger robot had come in. Now it presented its message respectfully to Wisdom. "From analysis, sir."

Wisdom tore the tape open. "Now we'll know how it thinks." His hands were shaking. "Maybe we can figure out its blind spot. It may be able to out-think us, but that doesn't mean it's invulnerable. It only predicts the future—it can't change it. If there's only death ahead, its ability won't . . ."

Wisdom's voice faded into silence. After a moment he passed the tape to Baines.

"I'll be down in the bar," Wisdom said. "Getting a good stiff drink." His face had turned lead-gray. "All I can say is *I hope to hell this isn't the race to come.*"

"What's the analysis?" Anita demanded impatiently, peering over Baines's shoulder. "How does it think?"

"It doesn't," Baines said, as he handed the tape back to his boss. "It doesn't think at all. Virtually no frontal lobe. It's not a human being—it doesn't use symbols. It's nothing but an animal."

"An animal," Wisdom said. "With a single highly developed faculty. Not a superior man. Not a man at all."

Up and down the corridors of the DCA Building, guards and equipment clanged. Loads of Civil Police were pouring into the building and taking up positions beside the guards. One by one, the corridors and rooms were being inspected and sealed off. Sooner or later the golden figure of Cris Johnson would be located and cornered.

"We were always afraid a mutant with superior intellectual powers would come along," Baines said reflectively. "A deeve who would be to us what we are to the great apes. Something with a bulging cranium, telepathic ability, a perfect semantic system, ultimate powers of symbolization and calculation. A development along our own path. A better human being."

"He acts by reflex," Anita said wonderingly. She had the analysis and was sitting at one of the desks studying it intently. "Reflex—like a lion. A golden lion." She pushed the tape aside, a strange expression on her face. "The lion god."

"Beast," Wisdom corrected tartly. "Blond beast, you mean."

"He runs fast," Baines said, "and that's all. No tools. He doesn't build anything or utilize anything outside himself. He just stands and waits for the right opportunity and then he runs like hell."

"This is worse than anything we've anticipated," Wisdom said. His beefy face was lead-gray. He sagged like an old man, his blunt hands trembling and uncertain. "To be replaced by an animal! Something that runs and hides. Something without a language!" He spat savagely. "That's why they weren't able to communicate with it. We wondered what kind of semantic system it had. It hasn't got any! No more ability to talk and think than a—dog."

"That means intelligence has failed," Baines went on huskily. "We're the last of our line—like the dinosaur. We've carried intelligence as far as it'll go. Too far, maybe. We've already got to the point where we know so much—think so much—we can't act."

"Men of thought," Anita said. "Not men of action. It's begun to have a paralyzing effect. But this thing—"

"This thing's faculty works better than ours ever did. We can recall past experiences, keep them in mind, learn from them. At best, we can make shrewd guesses about the future, from our memory of what's happened in the past. But we can't be certain. We have to speak of probabilities. Grays. Not blacks and whites. We're only guessing."

"Cris Johnson isn't guessing," Anita added.

"He can look ahead. See what's coming. He can—prethink. Let's call it that. He can see into the future. Probably he doesn't perceive it as the future."

"No," Anita said thoughtfully. "It would seem like the present. He has a broader present. But his present lies ahead, not back. Our present is related to the past. Only the past is certain, to us. To him, the future is certain. And he probably doesn't remember the past, any more than any animal remembers what's happened."

"As he develops," Baines said, "as his race evolves, it'll probably expand its ability to prethink. Instead of ten minutes, thirty minutes. Then an hour. A day. A year. Eventually they'll be able to keep ahead a whole lifetime. Each one of them will live in a solid, unchanging world. There'll be no variables, no uncertainty. No motion! They won't have anything to fear. Their world will be perfectly static, a solid block of matter."

"And when death comes," Anita said, "they'll accept it. There won't be any struggle; to them, it'll already have happened."

"*Already have happened,*" Baines repeated. "To Cris, our shots had already been fired." He laughed harshly. "Superior survival doesn't mean superior man. If there were another world-wide flood, only fish would survive. If there were another ice age, maybe nothing but polar bears would be left. When we opened the lock, he had already seen the men, seen exactly where they were standing and what they'd do. A neat faculty—but not a development of mind. A pure physical *sense.*"

"But if every exit is covered," Wisdom repeated, "he'll see he can't get out. He gave himself up before—he'll give himself up again." He shook his head. "An animal. Without language. Without tools."

"With his new sense," Baines said, "he doesn't need anything else." He examined his watch. "It's after two. Is the building completely sealed off?"

"You can't leave," Wisdom stated. "You'll have to stay here all night—or until we catch the bastard."

"I meant her." Baines indicated Anita. "She's supposed to be back at Semantics by seven in the morning."

Wisdom shrugged. "I have no control over her. If she wants, she can check out."

"I'll stay," Anita decided. "I want to be here when he—when he's destroyed. I'll sleep here." She hesitated. "Wisdom, isn't there some other way? If he's just an animal, couldn't we—"

"A zoo?" Wisdom's voice rose in a frenzy of hysteria. "Keep it penned up in the zoo? Christ, no! It's got to be killed!"

For a long time the great gleaming shape crouched in the darkness. He was in a store room. Boxes and cartons stretched out on all sides, heaped up in orderly rows, all neatly counted and marked. Silent and deserted.

But in a few moments people would burst in and search the room. He could see this. He saw them in all parts of the room, clear and distinct, men with lash-tubes, grim-faced, stalking with murder in their eyes.

The sight was one of many. One of a multitude of clearly etched scenes lying tangent to his own. And to each was attached a further multitude of interlocking scenes, that finally grew hazier and dwindled away. A progressive vagueness, each syndrome less distinct.

But the immediate one, the scene that lay closest to him, was clearly visible. He could easily make out the sight of the armed men. Therefore it was necessary to be out of the room before they appeared.

The golden figure got calmly to its feet and moved to the door. The corridor was empty; he could see himself already outside, in the vacant, drumming hall of metal and recessed lights. He pushed the door boldly open and stepped out.

A lift blinked across the hall. He walked to the lift and entered it. In five minutes a group of guards would come running along and leap into the lift. By that time he would have left it and sent it back down. Now he pressed a button and rose to the next floor.

He stepped out into a deserted passage. No one was in sight. That didn't surprise him. He couldn't be surprised. The element didn't exist for him. The positions of things, the space relationships of all matter in the immediate future, were as certain for him as his own body. The only thing that was unknown was that which had already passed out of being. In a vague, dim fashion, he had occasionally wondered where things went after he had passed them.

He came to a small supply closet. It had just been searched. It would be half an hour before anyone opened it again. He had that long; he could see that far ahead. And then—

And then he would be able to see another area, a region farther beyond. He was always moving, advancing into new regions he had never seen before. A constantly unfolding panorama of sights and scenes, frozen landscapes spread out ahead. All objects were fixed. Pieces on a vast chessboard through which he moved, arms folded, face calm. A detached observer who saw objects that lay ahead of him as clearly as those under foot.

Right now, as he crouched in the small supply closet, he saw an unusually varied multitude of scenes for the next half hour. Much lay ahead. The half hour was divided into an incredibly complex pattern of separate configurations. He had reached a critical region; he was about to move through worlds of intricate complexity.

He concentrated on a scene ten minutes away. It showed, like a three-dimensional still, a heavy gun at the end of the corridor, trained all the way to the far end. Men moved cautiously from door to door, checking each room again, as they had done repeatedly. At the end of the half hour they had reached the supply closet. A scene showed them looking inside. By that time he was gone, of course. He wasn't in that scene. He had passed on to another.

The next scene showed an exit. Guards stood in a solid line. No way out. He was in that scene. Off to one side, in a niche just inside the door. The street outside was visible, stars, lights, outlines of passing cars and people.

In the next tableau he had gone back, away from the exit. There was no way out. In another tableau he saw himself at other exits, a legion of golden figures, duplicated again and again, as he explored regions ahead, one after another. But each exit was covered.

In one dim scene he saw himself lying charred and dead; he had tried to run through the line, out the exit.

But that scene was vague. One wavering, indistinct still out of many. The inflexible path along which he moved would not deviate in that direction. It would not turn him that way. The golden figure in that scene, the miniature doll in that room, was only distantly related to him. It was himself, but a faraway self. A self he would never meet. He forgot it and went on to examine the other tableau.

The myriad of tableaux that surrounded him were an elaborate maze, a web which he now considered bit by bit. He was looking down into a doll's house of infinite rooms, rooms without number, each with its furniture, its dolls, all rigid and unmoving. The same dolls and furniture were repeated in many. He, himself, appeared often. The two men on the platform. The woman. Again and again the same combinations turned up; the play was redone frequently, the same actors and props moved around in all possible ways.

Before it was time to leave the supply closet, Cris Johnson had examined each of the rooms tangent to the one he now occupied. He had consulted each, considered its contents thoroughly.

He pushed the door open and stepped calmly out into the hall. He knew exactly where he was going. And what he had to do. Crouched in the stuffy closet, he had quietly and expertly examined each miniature of himself, observed which clearly etched configuration lay along his inflexible path, the one room of the doll house, the one set out of legions, toward which he was moving.

Anita slipped out of her metal-foil dress, hung it over a hanger, then unfastened her shoes and kicked them under the bed. She was just starting to unclip her bra when the door opened.

She gasped. Soundlessly, calmly, the great golden shape closed the door and bolted it after him.

Anita snatched up her lash-tube from the dressing table. Her hand shook; her whole body was trembling. "What do you want?" she demanded. Her fingers tightened convulsively around the tube. "I'll kill you."

The figure regarded her silently, arms folded. It was the first time she had seen Cris Johnson closely. The great dignified face, handsome and impassive. Broad shoulders. The golden mane of hair, golden skin, pelt of radiant fuzz—

"Why?" she demanded breathlessly. Her heart was pounding wildly. "What do you want?"

She could kill him easily. But the lash-tube wavered. Cris Johnson stood without fear; he wasn't at all afraid. Why not? Didn't he understand what it was? What the small metal tube could do to him?

"Of course," she said suddenly, in a choked whisper. "You can see ahead. You know I'm not going to kill you. Or you wouldn't have come here."

She flushed, terrified—and embarrassed. He knew exactly what she was going to do; he could see it as easily as she saw the walls of the room, the wall-bed with its covers folded neatly back, her clothes hanging in the closet, her purse and small things on the dressing table.

"All right." Anita backed away, then abruptly put the tube down on the dressing table. "I won't kill you. Why should I?" She fumbled in her purse and got out her cigarettes. Shakily, she lit up, her pulse racing. She was scared. And strangely fascinated. "Do you expect to stay here? It won't do any good. They've come through the dorm twice, already. They'll be back."

Could he understand her? She saw nothing on his face, only blank dignity. God, he was huge! It wasn't possible he was only eighteen, a boy, a child. He looked more like some great golden god, come down to earth.

She shook the thought off savagely. He wasn't a god. He was a beast. *The blond beast,* come to take the place of man. To drive man from the earth.

Anita snatched up the lash-tube. "Get out of here! You're an animal! A big stupid animal! You can't even understand what I'm saying—you don't even have a language. You're not human."

Cris Johnson remained silent. As if he were waiting. Waiting for what? He showed no sign of fear or impatience, even though the corridor outside rang with the sound of men searching, metal against metal, guns and energy tubes being dragged around, shouts and dim rumbles as section after section of the building was searched and sealed off.

"They'll get you," Anita said. "You'll be trapped here. They'll be searching this wing at any moment." She savagely stubbed out her cigarette. "For God's sake, what do you expect *me* to do?"

Cris moved toward her. Anita shrank back. His powerful hands caught hold of her and she gasped in sudden terror. For a moment she struggled blindly, desperately.

"Let go!" She broke away and leaped back from him. His face was expressionless. Calmly, he came toward her, an impassive god advancing to take her. "Get away!" She groped for the lash-tube, trying to get it up. But the tube slipped from her fingers and rolled onto the floor.

Cris bent down and picked it up. He held it out to her, in the open palm of his hand.

"Good God," Anita whispered. Shakily, she accepted the tube, gripped it hesitantly, then put it down again on the dressing table.

In the half-light of the room, the great golden figure seemed to glow and shimmer, outlined against the darkness. A god—no, not a god. An animal. A great golden beast, without a soul. She was confused. Which was he—or was he both? She shook her head, bewildered. It was late, almost four. She was exhausted and confused.

Cris took her in his arms. Gently, kindly, he lifted her face and kissed her. His powerful hands held her tight. She couldn't breathe. Darkness, mixed with the shimmering golden haze, swept around her. Around and around it spiraled, carrying her senses away. She sank down into it gratefully. The darkness covered her and dissolved her in a swelling torrent of sheer force that mounted in intensity each moment, until the roar of it beat against her and at last blotted out everything.

Anita blinked. She sat up and automatically pushed her hair into place. Cris was standing before the closet. He was reaching up, getting something down.

He turned toward her and tossed something on the bed. Her heavy metal-foil traveling cape.

Anita gazed down at the cape without comprehension. "What do you want?"

Cris stood by the bed, waiting.

She picked up the cape uncertainly. Cold creepers of fear plucked at her. "You want me to get you out of here," she said softly. "Past the guards and the CP."

Cris said nothing.

"They'll kill you instantly." She got unsteadily to her feet. "You can't run past them. Good God, don't you do anything but run? There must be a better way. Maybe I can appeal to Wisdom. I'm Class A—Director Class. I can go directly to the Full Directorate. I ought to be able to hold them off, keep back the euth indefinitely. The odds are a billion to one against us if we try to break past—"

She broke off.

"But you don't gamble," she continued slowly. "You don't go by odds. You *know* what's coming. You've seen the cards already." She studied his face intently. "No, you can't be cold-decked. It wouldn't be possible."

For a moment she stood deep in thought. Then with a quick, decisive motion, she snatched up the cloak and slipped it around her bare shoulders. She fastened the heavy belt, bent down and got her shoes from under the bed, snatched up her purse, and hurried to the door.

"Come on," she said. She was breathing quickly, cheeks flushed. "Let's go. While there are still a number of exits to choose from. My car is parked outside, in the lot at the side of the building. We can get to my place in an hour. I have a winter home in Argentina. If worst comes to worst, we can fly there. It's in the back country, away from the cities. Jungle and swamps. Cut off from almost everything." Eagerly, she started to open the door.

Cris reached out and stopped her. Gently, patiently, he moved in front of her.

He waited a long time, body rigid. Then he turned the knob and stepped boldly out into the corridor.

The corridor was empty. No one was in sight. Anita caught a faint glimpse, the back of a guard hurrying off. If they had come out a second earlier—

Cris started down the corridor. She ran after him. He moved rapidly, effortlessly. The girl had trouble keeping up with him. He seemed to know exactly where to go. Off to the right, down a side hall, a supply passage. Onto an ascent freight-lift. They rose, then abruptly halted.

Cris waited again. Presently he slid the door back and moved out of the lift. Anita followed nervously. She could hear sounds: guns and men, very close.

They were near an exit. A double line of guards stood directly ahead. Twenty men, a solid wall—and a massive heavy-duty robot gun in the center. The men were alert, faces strained and tense. Watching wide-eyed, guns gripped tight. A Civil Police officer was in charge.

"We'll never get past," Anita gasped. "We wouldn't get ten feet." She pulled back. "They'll—"

Cris took her by the arm and continued calmly forward. Blind terror leaped inside her. She fought wildly to get away, but his fingers were like steel. She couldn't pry them loose. Quietly, irresistibly, the great golden creature drew her along beside him, toward the double line of guards.

"There he is!" Guns went up. Men leaped into action. The barrel of the robot cannon swung around. *"Get him!"*

Anita was paralyzed. She sagged against the powerful body beside her, tugged along helplessly by his inflexible grasp. The lines of guards came nearer, a sheer wall of guns. Anita fought to control her terror. She stumbled, half fell. Cris supported her effortlessly. She scratched, fought at him, struggled to get loose—

"Don't shoot!" she screamed.

Guns wavered uncertainly. "Who is she?" The guards were moving around, trying to get a sight on Cris without including her. "Who's he got there?"

One of them saw the stripe on her sleeve. Red and black. Director Class. Top-level.

"She's Class A." Shocked, the guards retreated. "Miss, get out of the way!"

Anita found her voice. "Don't shoot. He's—in my custody. You understand? I'm taking him out."

The wall of guards moved back nervously. "No one's supposed to pass. Director Wisdom gave orders—"

"I'm not subject to Wisdom's authority." She managed to edge her voice with a harsh crispness. "Get out of the way. I'm taking him to a Semantics Agency."

For a moment nothing happened. There was no reaction. Then slowly, uncertainly, one guard stepped aside.

Cris moved. A blur of speed, away from Anita, past the confused guards, through the breach in the line, out the exit, and onto the street. Bursts of energy flashed wildly after him. Shouting guards milled out. Anita was left behind, forgotten. The guards, the heavy-duty gun, were pouring out into the early-morning darkness. Sirens wailed. Patrol cars roared into life.

Anita stood dazed, confused, leaning against the wall, trying to get her breath.

He was gone. He had left her. Good God—what had she done? She shook her head, bewildered, her face buried in her hands. She had been hypnotized. She had lost her will, her common sense. Her reason! The animal, the great golden beast, had tricked her. Taken advantage of her. And now he was gone, escaped into the night.

Miserable, agonized tears trickled through her clenched fingers. She rubbed at them futilely; but they kept on coming.

"He's gone," Baines said. "We'll never get him, now. He's probably a million miles from here."

Anita sat huddled in the corner, her face to the wall. A little bent heap, broken and wretched.

Wisdom paced back and forth. "But where can he go? Where can he hide? Nobody'll hide him! Everybody knows the law about deeves!"

"He's lived out in the woods most of his life. He'll hunt—that's what he's always done. They wondered what he was up to, off by himself. He was catching game and sleeping under trees." Baines laughed harshly. "And the first woman he meets will be glad to hide him—as *she* was." He indicated Anita with a jerk of his thumb.

"So all that gold, that mane, that godlike stance, was *for* something. Not just ornament." Wisdom's thick lips twisted. "He doesn't have just one faculty—he has two. One is new, the newest thing in survival methods. The other is as old as life." He stopped pacing to glare at the huddled shape in the corner. "Plumage. Bright feathers, combs for the roosters, swans, birds, bright scales for the fish. Gleaming pelts and manes for the animals. An animal isn't necessarily *bestial.* Lions aren't bestial. Or tigers. Or any of the big cats. They're anything but bestial."

"He'll never have to worry," Baines said. "He'll get by—as long as human women exist to take care of him. And since he can see ahead, into the future, he already knows he's sexually irresistible to human females."

"We'll get him," Wisdom muttered. "I've had the government declare an emergency. Military and Civil Police will be looking for him. Armies of men—a whole planet of experts, the most advanced machines and equipment. We'll flush him, sooner or later."

"By that time it won't make any difference," Baines said. He put his hand on Anita's shoulder and patted her ironically. "You'll have company, sweetheart. You won't be the only one. You're just the first of a long procession."

"Thanks," Anita grated.

"The oldest survival method and the newest. Combined to form one perfectly adapted animal. How the hell are we going to stop him? We can put *you* through a sterilization tank—but we can't pick them all up, all the women he meets along the way. And if we miss one we're finished."

"We'll have to keep trying," Wisdom said. "Round up as many as we can. Before they can spawn." Faint hope glinted in his tired, sagging face. "Maybe his characteristics are recessive. Maybe ours will cancel his out."

"I wouldn't lay any money on that," Baines said. "I think I know already which of the two strains is going to turn up dominant." He grinned wryly. "I mean, I'm making a good *guess.* It won't be us."

DANGER—HUMAN!

Gordon R. Dickson

Here is a different kind of superman—no mutant, nothing extraordinary at all about him, simply a human being—a superman whose special powers manifest themselves only under conditions of unusual stress. Gordon R. Dickson, for two decades one of science fiction's most popular authors, is a Hugo and Nebula winner and a past president of the Science Fiction Writers of America, whose best-known books include Soldier, Ask Not; Naked to the Stars; *and* None But Man. *He lives in Minnesota.*

The spaceboat came down in the silence of perfect working order—down through the cool, dark night of a New Hampshire late spring. There was hardly any moon and the path emerging from the clump of conifers and snaking its way across the dim pasture looked like a long strip of pale cloth, carelessly dropped and forgotten there.

The two aliens checked the boat and stopped it, hovering, some fifty feet above the pasture, and all but invisible against the low-lying clouds. Then they set themselves to wait, their woolly, bearlike forms settled on haunches, their uniform belts glinting a little in the shielded light from the instrument panel, talking now and then in desultory murmurs.

"It's not a bad place," said the one of junior rank, looking down at the earth below.

"Why should it be?" answered the senior.

The junior did not answer. He shifted on his haunches.

"The babies are due soon," he said. "I just got a message."

"How many?" asked the senior.

"Three—the doctor thinks. That's not bad for a first birthing."

"My wife only had two."

"I know. You told me."

They fell silent for a few seconds. The spaceboat rocked almost imperceptibly in the waters of night.

"Look—" said the junior, suddenly. "Here it comes, right on schedule."

The senior glanced overside. Down below, a tall, dark form had emerged from the trees and was coming out along the path. A little beam of light shone before him, terminating in a blob of illumination that danced along the path ahead, lighting his way. The senior stiffened.

"Take controls," he said. The casualness had gone out of his voice. It had become crisp, impersonal.

"Controls," answered the other, in the same emotionless voice.

"Take her down."

"Down it is."

The spaceboat dropped groundward. There was an odd sort of soundless, lightless explosion—it was as if a concussive wave had passed, robbed of all effects but one. The figure dropped, the light rolling from its grasp and losing its glow in a tangle of short grass. The spaceboat landed and the two aliens got out.

In the dark night they loomed furrily above the still figure. It was that of a lean, dark man in his early thirties, dressed in clean, much-washed corduroy pants and checkered wool lumberjack shirt. He was unconscious, but breathing slowly, deeply and easily.

"I'll take it up by the head, here," said the senior. "You take the other end. Got it? Lift! Now, carry it into the boat."

The junior backed away, up through the spaceboat's open lock, grunting a little with the awkwardness of his burden.

"It feels slimy," he said.

"Nonsense!" said the senior. "That's your imagination."

Eldridge Timothy Parker drifted in that dreamy limbo between awakeness and full sleep. He found himself contemplating his own name.

Eldridge Timothy Parker. Eldridgetimothyparker. Eldridge-TIMOTHYparker. ELdrIDGEtiMothyPARKer. . . .

There was a hardness under his back, the back on which he was lying—and a coolness. His flaccid right hand turned flat, feeling. It felt like steel beneath him. Metal? He tried to sit up and bumped his forehead against a ceiling a few inches overhead. He blinked his eyes in the darkness—

Darkness?

He flung out his hands, searching, feeling terror leap up inside him. His knuckles bruised against walls to right and left. Frantic, his groping fingers felt out, around and about him. He was walled in, he was surrounded, he was enclosed.

Completely.

Like in a coffin.

Buried—

He began to scream. . . .

Much later, when he awoke again, he was in a strange place that seemed to have no walls, but many instruments. He floated in the center of mechanisms that passed and repassed about him, touching, probing, turning. He felt touches of heat and cold. Strange hums and notes of various pitches came and went. He felt voices questioning him.

Who are you?

"Eldridge Parker—Eldridge Timothy Parker—"

What are you?

"I'm Eldridge Parker—"

Tell about yourself.

"Tell what? What?"

Tell about yourself.

"What? What do you want to know? What—"

Tell about. . . .

"But I—"

Tell. . . .

. . . well, i suppose i was pretty much like any of the kids around our town . . . i was a pretty good shot and i won the fifth-grade seventy-five-yard dash . . . i played hockey, too . . . pretty cold weather up around our parts, you know, the air used to smell strange it was so cold winter mornings in january when you first stepped out of doors . . . it is good, open country, new england, and there were lots of smells . . . there were pine smells and grass smells and i remember especially the kitchen smells . . . and then, too, there was the way the oak benches in church used to smell on sunday when you knelt with your nose right next to the back of the pew ahead. . . .

. . . the fishing up our parts is good too . . . i liked to fish but i never wasted time on weekdays . . . we were presbyterians, you know, and my father had the farm, but he also had money invested in land around the country . . . we have never been badly off but i would have liked a motorscooter. . . .

. . . no i did not never hate the germans, at least i did not think i ever did, of course though i was over in europe i never really had it bad, combat, i mean . . . i was in a motor pool with the raw smell of gasoline, i like to work with my hands, and it was not like being in the infantry. . . .

. . . i have as good right to speak up to the town council as any man . . . i do not believe in pushing but if they push me i am going to push right back . . . nor it isn't any man's business what i voted last election no more than my bank balance . . . but i have got as good a right to a say in town doings as if i was the biggest landholder among them. . . .

. . . i did not go to college because it was not necessary . . . too much education can make a fool of any man, i told my father, and i know when i have had enough . . . i am a farmer and will always be a farmer and i will do my own studying as things come up without taking out a pure waste of four years to hang a piece of paper on the wall. . . .

. . . of course i know about the atom bomb, but i am no scientist and no need to be one, no more than i need to be a veterinarian . . . i elect the men that hire the men that need to know those things and the men that i elect will hear from me johnny-quick if things do not go to my liking. . . .

. . . as to why i never married, that is none of your business . . . as it happens, i was never at ease with women much, though there were a couple of times, and i still may if jeanie lind. . . .

. . . i believe in god and the united states of america. . . .

He woke up gradually. He was in a room that might have been any office, except the furniture was different. That is, there was a box with doors on it that might have been a filing cabinet and a table that looked like a desk in spite of the single thin rod underneath the center that supported it. However, there were no chairs —only small, flat cushions, on which three large woolly, bearlike creatures were sitting and watching him in silence.

He himself, he found, was in a chair, though.

As soon as they saw his eyes were open, they turned away from him and began to talk among themselves. Eldridge Parker shook his head and blinked his eyes, and would have blinked his ears if that had been possible. For the sounds the creatures were making were like nothing he had ever heard before; and yet he understood everything they were saying. It was an odd sensation, like a double image earwise, for he heard the strange mouth-noises just as they came out and then something in his head twisted them around and made them into perfectly understandable English.

Nor was that all. For, as he sat listening to the creatures talk, he began to get the same double image in another way. That is, he still saw the bearlike creature behind the desk as the weird sort of animal he was, but out of the sound of his voice, or from something else, there gradually built up in Eldridge's mind a picture of a thin, rather harassed-looking gray-haired man in something resembling a uniform, but at the same time not quite a uniform. It was the sort of effect an army general might get if he wore his stars and a Sam Browne belt over a civilian double-breasted suit. Similarly, the other creature sitting facing the one behind the desk, at the desk's side, was a young and black-haired man with something of the laboratory about him, and the creature farther back, seated almost against the wall, was neither soldier nor scientist, but a heavy older man with a sort of book-won wisdom in him.

"You see, commander," the young one with the black-haired image was saying, "perfectly restored. At least on the physical and mental levels."

"Good, Doctor, good," the outlandish syllables from the one behind the desk translated themselves in Eldridge's head. "And you say it . . . he, I should say . . . will be able to understand?"

"Certainly, sir," said the doctor-psychologist-whatever-he-was. "Identification is absolute—"

"But I mean comprehend—encompass—" The creature behind the desk moved one paw slightly. "Follow what we tell him—"

The doctor turned his ursinoid head toward the third member of the group. This one spoke slowly, in a deeper voice.

"The culture allows. Certainly."

The one behind the desk bowed slightly to the oldest one. "Certainly, Academician, certainly."

They then fell silent, all looking back at Eldridge, who returned their gaze with equivalent interest. There was something unnatural about the whole proceeding. Each side was regarding the other with the completely blunt and unshielded curiosity given to freaks.

The silence stretched out. It became tinged with a certain embarrassment. Gradually a mutual recognition arose that no one really wanted to be the first to address an alien being directly.

"It . . . he is comfortable?" asked the commander, turning once more to the doctor.

"I should say so," replied the doctor, slowly. "As far as we know. . . ."

Turning back to Eldridge, the commander said, "Eldridgetimothyparker, I suppose you wonder where you are?"

Caution and habit put a clamp on Eldridge's tongue. He hesitated about answering so long that the commander turned in distress to the doctor, who reassured him with a slight movement of the head.

"Well, speak up," said the commander, "we'll be able to understand you, just as you're able to understand us. Nothing's going to hurt you; and anything you say won't have the slightest effect on your . . . er . . . situation."

He paused again, looking at Eldridge for a comment. Eldridge still held his silence, but one of his hands unconsciously made a short, fumbling motion at his breast pocket.

"My pipe—" said Eldridge.

The three looked at each other. They looked back at Eldridge.

"We have it," said the doctor. "After a while we may give it back to you. For now . . . we cannot allow . . . it would not suit us."

"Smoke bothers you?" said Eldridge, with a touch of his native canniness.

"It does not bother us. It is . . . merely . . . distasteful," said the commander. "Let's get on. I'm going to tell you where you are, first. You're on a world roughly similar to your own, but many . . ." he hesitated, looking at the academician.

"Light-years," supplemented the deep voice.

". . . Light-years in terms of what a year means to you," went on the commander, with growing briskness. "Many light-years distant from your home. We didn't bring you here because of any personal . . . dislike . . . or enmity for you; but for . . ."

"Observation," supplied the doctor. The commander turned and bowed slightly to him, and was bowed back at in return.

". . . Observation," went on the commander. "Now, do you understand what I've told you so far?"

"I'm listening," said Eldridge.

"Very well," said the commander. "I will go on. There is something about your people that we are very anxious to discover. We have been, and intend to continue, studying you to find it out. So far—I will admit quite frankly and freely—we have not found it; and the consensus among our best minds is that you, yourself, do not know what it is. Accordingly, we have hopes of . . . causing . . . you to discover it for yourself. And for us."

"Hey . . ." breathed Eldridge.

"Oh, you will be well treated. I assure you," said the commander, hurriedly. "You have been well treated. You have been . . . but you did not know . . . I mean you did not feel—"

"Can you remember any discomfort since we picked you up?" asked the doctor, leaning forward.

"Depends what you mean—"

"And you will feel none." The doctor turned to the commander. "Perhaps I'm getting ahead of myself?"

"Perhaps," said the commander. He bowed and turned back to Eldridge. "To explain—we hope you will discover our answer for it. We're only going to put you in a position to work on it. Therefore, we've decided to tell you everything. First—the problem. Academician?"

The oldest one bowed. His deep voice made the room ring oddly.

"If you will look this way," he said. Eldridge turned his head. The other raised one paw and the wall beside him dissolved into a maze of lines and points. "Do you know what this is?"

"No," said Eldridge.

"It is," rumbled the one called the academician, "a map of the known universe. You lack the training to read it in four dimensions, as it should be read. No matter. You will take my word for it . . . it is a map. A map covering hundreds of thousands of your light-years and millions of your years."

He looked at Eldridge, who said nothing.

"To go on, then, What we know of your race is based upon two sources of information. History. And legend. The history is sketchy. It rests on archaeological discoveries for the most part. The legend is even sketchier and—fantastic."

He paused again. Still Eldridge guarded his tongue.

"Briefly, there is a race that has three times broken out to overrun this mapped area of our galaxy and dominate other civilized cultures—until some inherent lack or weakness in the individual caused the component parts of this advance to die out. The periods of these outbreaks have always been disastrous for the dominated cultures and uniformly without benefit to the race I am talking about. In the case of each outbreak, though the home planet was destroyed and all known remnants of the advancing race hunted out, unknown seed communities remained to furnish the material for a new advance some thousands of years later. That race," said the academician, and coughed—or at least made some kind of noise in his throat, "is your own."

Eldridge watched the other carefully and without moving.

"We see your race, therefore," went on the academician, and Eldridge received the mental impression of an elderly man putting the tips of his fingers together judiciously, "as one with great or overwhelming natural talents, but unfortunately also with one great natural flaw. This flaw seems to be a desire—almost a need—to acquire and possess things. To reach out, encompass, and absorb. It is not," shrugged the academician, "a unique trait. Other races have it—but not to such an extent that it makes them a threat to their co-existing cultures. Yet, this in itself is not the real problem. If it was a simple matter of rapacity, a combination of other races should be able to contain your people. There is a natural inevitable balance of that sort continually at work in the galaxy. No," said the academician, and paused, looking at the commander.

"Go on. Go on," said the commander. The academician bowed.

"No, it is not that simple. As a guide to what remains, we have only the legend, made anew and reinforced after each outward sweep of your people. We know that there must be something more than we have found—and we have studied you carefully, both your home world and now you, personally. There *must* be something more in you, some genius, some capability above the normal, to account for the fantastic nature of your race's previous successes. But the legend says only—*Danger, Human! High Explosive. Do not touch*—and we find nothing in you to justify the warning."

He sighed. Or at least Eldridge received a sudden, unexpected intimation of deep weariness.

"Because of a number of factors—too numerous to go into and most of them not understandable to you—it is our race which must deal with this problem for the rest of the galaxy. What can we do? We dare not leave you be until you grow strong and come out once more. And the legend expressly warns us against touching you in any way. So we have chosen to pick one—but I intrude upon your field, Doctor."

The two of them exchanged bows. The doctor took up the talk, speaking briskly and entirely to Eldridge.

"A joint meeting of those of us best suited to consider the situation recommended that we pick up one specimen for intensive observation. For reasons of availability, you were the one chosen. Following your return under drugs to this planet, you were thoroughly examined, by the best of medical techniques, both mentally and physically. I will not go into detail, since we have no wish to depress you unduly. I merely want to impress on you the fact that we found nothing. Nothing. No unusual power or ability of any sort, such as history shows you to have had and legend hints at. I mention this because of the further course of action we have decided to take. Commander?"

The being behind the desk got to his hind feet. The other two rose.

"You will come with us," said the commander.

Herded by them, Eldridge went out through the room's door into brilliant sunlight and across a small stretch of something like concrete to a stubby egg-shaped craft with ridiculous little wings.

"Inside," said the commander. They got in. The commander squatted before a bank of instruments, manipulated a simple sticklike control, and after a moment the ship took to the air. They flew for perhaps half an hour, with Eldridge wishing he were in a position to see out one of the high windows, then landed at a field apparently literally hacked out of a small forest of mountains.

Crossing this field on foot, Eldridge got a glimpse of some truly huge ships, as well as a number of smaller ones such as the one in which he had arrived. Numbers of the furry aliens moved about, none with any great air of hurry, but all with purposefulness. There was a sudden, single, thunderous sound that was gone almost before the ear could register it; and Eldridge, who had ducked instinctively, looked up again to see one of the huge ships falling—there is no other word for it—skyward with such unbelievable rapidity it was out of sight in seconds.

The four of them came at last to a shallow, open trench in the stuff which made the field surface. It was less than a foot wide and they stepped across it with ease. But once they had crossed it, Eldridge noticed a difference. In the five-hundred-yard square enclosed by the trench—for it turned at right angles off to his right and to his left—there was an air of tightly established desertedness, as of some highly restricted area, and the rectangular concrete-looking building that occupied the square's very center glittered unoccupied in the clear light.

They marched to the door of this building and it opened without any of them touching it. Inside were perhaps twenty feet of floor, stretching inward as a rim inside the walls. Then a sort of moat—Eldridge could not see its depth—filled with a dark fluid with a faint, sharp odor. This was perhaps another twenty feet wide and enclosed a small, flat island perhaps fifteen feet by fifteen feet, almost wholly taken up by a cage whose walls and ceiling appeared to be made of metal bars as thick as a man's thumb and spaced about six inches apart. Two more of the aliens, wearing a sort of harness and holding a short, black tube apiece, stood on the ledge of the outer rim. A temporary bridge had been laid across the moat, protruding through the open door of the cage.

They all went across the bridge and into the cage. There, standing around rather like a board of directors viewing an addition to the company plant, they faced Eldridge; and the commander spoke.

"This will be your home from now on," he said. He indicated the cot, the human-type chair and the other items furnishing the cage. "It's as comfortable as we can make it."

"Why?" burst out Eldridge, suddenly. "Why're you locking me up here? Why—"

"In our attempt to solve the problem that still exists," interrupted the doctor, smoothly, "we can do nothing more than keep you under observation and hope that time will work with us. Also, we hope to influence you to search for the solution, yourself."

"And if I find it—what?" cried Eldridge.

"Then," said the commander, "we will deal with you in the kindest manner that the solution permits. It may be even possible to return you to your own world. At the very least, once you are no longer needed, we can see to it that you are quickly and painlessly destroyed."

Eldridge felt his insides twist within him.

"Kill me?" he choked. "You think that's going to make me help you? The hope of getting killed?"

They looked at him almost compassionately.

"You may find," said the doctor, "that death may be something you will want very much, only for the purpose of putting a close to a life you've become weary of. Look"—he gestured around him —"you are locked up beyond any chance of ever escaping. This cage will be illuminated night and day; and you will be locked in it. When we leave, the bridge will be withdrawn, and the only thing crossing that moat—which is filled with acid—will be a mechanical arm which will extend across and through a small opening to bring you food twice a day. Beyond the moat, there will be two armed guards on duty at all times, but even they cannot open the door to this building. That is opened by remote control from outside, only after the operator has checked on his vision screen to make sure all is as it should be inside here."

He gestured through the bars, across the moat and through a window in the outer wall.

"Look out there," he said.

Eldridge looked. Out beyond, and surrounding the building, the shallow trench no longer lay still and empty under the sun. It now spouted a vertical wall of flickering, weaving distortion, like a barrier of heat waves.

"That is our final defense, the ultimate in destructiveness that our science provides us—it would literally burn you to nothingness, if you touched it. It will be turned off only for seconds, and with elaborate precautions, to let guards in, or out."

Eldridge looked back in, to see them all watching him.

"We do this," said the doctor, "not only because we may discover you to be more dangerous than you seem, but to impress you with your helplessness so that you may be more ready to help *us*. Here you are, and here you will stay."

"And you think," demanded Eldridge hoarsely, "that this's all going to make me want to help you?"

"Yes," said the doctor, "because there's one thing more that enters into the situation. You were literally taken apart physically, after your capture; and as literally put back together again. We are advanced in the organic field, and certain things are true of all life forms. I supervised the work on you, myself. You will find that you are, for all practical purposes, immortal and irretrievably sane. This will be your home forever, and you will find that neither death nor insanity will provide you a way of escape."

They turned and filed out. From some remote control, the cage door was swung shut. He heard it click and lock. The bridge was withdrawn from the moat. A screen lit up and a woolly face surveyed the building's interior.

The building's door opened. They went out; and the guards took up their patrol, around the rim in opposite directions, keeping their eyes on Eldridge and their weapons ready in their hands. The building's door closed again. Outside, the flickering wall blinked out for a second and then returned again.

The silence of a warm, summer, mountain afternoon descended upon the building. The footsteps of the guards made shuffling noises on their path around the rim. The bars enclosed him.

Eldridge stood still, holding the bars in both hands and looking out.

He could not believe it.

He could not believe it as the days piled up into weeks, and the weeks into months. But as the seasons shifted and the year came around to a new year, the realities of his situation began to soak into him like water into a length of dock piling. For outside, Time could be seen at its visible and regular motion; but in his prison, there was no Time.

Always the lights burned overhead, always the guards paced about him. Always the barrier burned beyond the building, the meals came swinging in on the end of a long metal arm extended over the moat and through a small hatchway which opened automatically as the arm approached; regularly, twice weekly, the doctor came and checked him over, briefly, impersonally—and went out again with the changing of the guard.

He felt the unbearableness of his situation, like a hand winding tighter and tighter day by day the spring of tension within him. He took to pacing feverishly up and down the cage. He went back and forth, back and forth, until the room swam. He lay awake nights, staring at the endless glow of illumination from the ceiling. He rose to pace again.

The doctor came and examined him. He talked to Eldridge, but Eldridge would not answer. Finally there came a day when everything split wide open and he began to howl and bang on the bars. The guards were frightened and called the doctor. The doctor came, and with two others, entered the cage and strapped him down. They did something odd that hurt at the back of his neck and he passed out.

When he opened his eyes again, the first thing he saw was the doctor's woolly face, looking down at him—he had learned to recognize that countenance in the same way a sheep-herder eventually comes to recognize individual sheep in his flock. Eldridge felt very weak, but calm.

"You tried hard—" said the doctor. "But you see, you didn't make it. There's no way out *that* way for you."

Eldridge smiled.

"Stop that!" said the doctor sharply. "You aren't fooling us. We know you're perfectly rational."

Eldridge continued to smile.

"What do you think you're doing?" demanded the doctor. Eldridge looked happily up at him.

"I'm going home," he said.

"I'm sorry," said the doctor. "You don't convince me." He turned and left. Eldridge turned over on his side and dropped off into the first good sleep he'd had in months.

In spite of himself, however, the doctor was worried. He had the guards doubled, but nothing happened. The days slipped into weeks again and nothing happened. Eldridge was apparently fully recovered. He still spent a great deal of time walking up and down his cage and grasping the bars as if to pull them out of the way before him—but the frenzy of his earlier pacing was gone. He had also moved his cot over next to the small, two-foot-square hatch that opened to admit the mechanical arm bearing his meals, and would lie there, with his face pressed against it, waiting for the food to be delivered. The doctor felt uneasy, and spoke to the commander privately about it.

"Well," said the commander, "just what is it you suspect?"

"I don't know," confessed the doctor. "It's just that I see him more frequently than any of us. Perhaps I've become sensitized—but he bothers me."

"Bothers you?"

"Frightens me, perhaps. I wonder if we've taken the right way with him."

"We took the only way." The commander made the little gesture and sound that was his race's equivalent of a sigh. "We must have data. What do you do when you run across a possibly dangerous virus, Doctor? You isolate it—for study, until you know. It is not possible, and too risky, to try to study his race at close hand, so we study him. That's all we're doing. You lose objectivity, Doctor. Would you like to take a short vacation?"

"No," said the doctor, slowly. "No. But he frightens me."

Still, time went on and nothing happened. Eldridge paced his cage and lay on his cot, face pressed to the bars of the hatch, and staring at the outside world. Another year passed; and another. The double guards were withdrawn. The doctor came reluctantly to the conclusion that the human had at last accepted the fact of his confinement and felt growing within him that normal sort of sympathy that feeds on familiarity. He tried to talk to Eldridge on his regularly scheduled visits, but Eldridge showed little interest in conversation. He lay on the cot watching the doctor as the doctor examined him, with something in his eyes as if he looked on from some distant place in which all decisions were already made and finished.

"You're as healthy as ever," said the doctor, concluding his examination. He regarded Eldridge. "I wish you would, though . . ." He broke off. "We aren't a cruel people, you know. We don't like the necessity that makes us do this."

He paused. Eldridge considered him without stirring.

"If you'd accept that fact," said the doctor, "I'm sure you'd make it easier on yourself. Possibly our figures of speech have given you a false impression. We said you are immortal. Well, of course, that's not true. Only practically speaking, are you immortal. You are now capable of living a very, very, very long time. That's all."

He paused again. After a moment of waiting, he went on.

"Just the same way, this business isn't really intended to go on for eternity. By its very nature, of course, it can't. Even races have a finite lifetime. But even that would be too long. No, it's just a matter of a long time as you might live it. Eventually, everything must come to a conclusion—that's inevitable."

Eldridge still did not speak. The doctor sighed.

"Is there anything you'd like?" he said. "We'd like to make this as little unpleasant as possible. Anything we can give you?"

Eldridge opened his mouth.

"Give me a boat," he said. "I want a fishing rod. I want a bottle of applejack."

The doctor shook his head sadly. He turned and signaled the guards. The cage door opened. He went out.

"Get me some pumpkin pie," cried Eldridge after him, sitting up on the cot and grasping the bars as the door closed. "Give me some green grass in here."

The doctor crossed the bridge. The bridge was lifted up and the monitor screen lit up. A woolly face looked out and saw that all was well. Slowly the outer door swung open.

"Get me some pine trees!" yelled Eldridge at the doctor's retreating back. "Get me some plowed fields! Get me some earth, some dirt, some plain, earth dirt! *Get me that!*"

The door shut behind the doctor; and Eldridge burst into

laughter, clinging to the bars, hanging there with flowing eyes.

"I would like to be relieved of this job," said the doctor to the commander, appearing formally in the latter's office.

"I'm sorry," said the commander. "I'm very sorry. But it was our tactical team that initiated this action; and no one has the experience with the prisoner you have. I'm sorry."

The doctor bowed his head; and went out.

Certain mild but emotion-deadening drugs were also known to the woolly, bearlike race. The doctor went out and began to indulge in them. Meanwhile, Eldridge lay on his cot, occasionally smiling to himself. His position was such that he could see out the window and over the weaving curtain of the barrier that ringed his building, to the landing field. After a while one of the large ships landed and when he saw the three members of its crew disembark from it and move, antlike, off across the field toward the buildings at its far end, he smiled again.

He settled back and closed his eyes. He seemed to doze for a couple of hours and then the sound of the door opening to admit the extra single guard bearing the food for his three o'clock mid-afternoon feeding. He sat up, pushed the cot down a ways, and sat on the end of it, waiting for the meal.

The bridge was not extended—that happened only when someone physically was to enter his cage. The monitor screen lit up and a woolly face watched as the tray of food was loaded on the mechanical arm. It swung out across the acid-filled moat, stretched itself toward the cage, and under the vigilance of the face in the monitor, the two-foot-square hatch opened just before it to let it extend into the cage.

Smiling, Eldridge took the tray. The arm withdrew; as it cleared the cage, the hatch swung shut and locked. Outside the cage, guards, food carrier, and face in the monitor relaxed. The food carrier turned toward the door, the face in the monitor looked down at some invisible control board before it, and the outer door swung open.

In that moment, Eldridge moved.

In one swift second he was on his feet and his hands had closed around the bars of the hatch. There was a single screech of metal, as—incredibly—he tore it loose and threw it aside. Then he was diving through the hatch opening.

He rolled head over heels like a gymnast and came up with his feet standing on the inner edge of the moat. The acrid scent of the acid faintly burnt at his nostrils. He sprang forward in a standing jump, arms outstretched—and his clutching fingers closed on the end of the food arm, now halfway in the process of its leisurely mechanical retraction across the moat.

The metal creaked and bent, dipping downward toward the acid, but Eldridge was already swinging onward under the powerful impetus of his arms, from which the sleeves had fallen back to reveal bulging ropes of smooth, powerful muscle. He flew forward through the air, feet first, and his boots took the nearest guard in the face, so that they crashed to the ground together.

For a second they rolled entangled, then the guard flopped and Eldridge came up on one knee, holding the black tube of the guard's weapon. It spat a single tongue of flame and the other guard dropped. Eldridge thrust to his feet, turning to the still-open door.

The door was closing. But the panicked food-carrier, unarmed, had turned to run. A bolt from Eldridge's weapon took him in the back. He fell forward and the door jammed on his body. Leaping after him, Eldridge squeezed through the remaining opening.

Then he was out under the free sky. The sounds of alarm screechers were splitting the air. He began to run—

The doctor was already drugged—but not so badly that he could not make it to the field when the news came. Driven by a strange perversity of spirit, he went first to the prison to inspect the broken hatch and the bent food arm. He traced Eldridge's outward path and it led him to the landing field, where he found the commander and the academician by a bare, darkened area of concrete. They acknowledged his presence by little bows.

"He took a ship here?" said the doctor.

"He took a ship here," said the commander.

There was a little silence between them.

"Well," said the academician, "we have been answered."

"Have we?" the commander looked at them almost appealingly. "There's no chance—that it was just chance? No chance that the hatch just happened to fail—and he acted without thinking, and was lucky?"

The doctor shook his head. He felt a little dizzy and unnatural from the drug, but the ordinary processes of his thinking were unimpaired.

"The hinges of the hatch," he said, "were rotten—eaten away by acid."

"Acid?" the commander stared at him. "Where would he get acid?"

"From his own digestive processes—regurgitated and spat directly into the hinges. He secreted hydrochloric acid among other things. Not too powerful—but over a period of time. . . ."

"Still—" said the commander, desperately, "I think it must have been more luck than otherwise."

"Can you believe that?" asked the academician. "Consider the timing of it all, the choosing of a moment when the food arm was in the proper position, the door open at the proper angle, the guard in a vulnerable situation. Consider his unhesitating and sure use of a weapon—which could only be the fruits of hours of observation, his choice of a moment when a fully supplied ship, its drive unit not yet cooled down, was waiting for him on the field. No," he shook his woolly head, "we have been answered. We put him in an escape-proof prison and he escaped."

"But none of this was possible," cried the commander.

The doctor laughed, a fuzzy, drug-blurred laugh. He opened his mouth but the academician was before him.

"It's not what he did," said the academician, "but the fact that he did it. No member of another culture that we know would have even entertained the possibility in its mind. Don't you see—he disregarded, he denied the fact that escape was impossible. *That* is what makes his kind so fearful, so dangerous. The fact that something is impossible presents no barrier to their seeking minds. That, alone, places them above us on a plane we can never reach."

"But it's a false premise!" protested the commander. "They cannot contravene natural laws. They are still bound by the physical order of the universe."

The doctor laughed again. His laugh had a wild quality. The commander looked at him.

"You're drugged," he said.

"Yes," choked the doctor. "And I'll be more drugged. I toast the end of our race, our culture, and our order."

"Hysteria!" said the commander.

"Hysteria?" echoed the doctor. "No—*guilt!* Didn't we do it, we three? The legend told us not to touch them, not to set a spark to the explosive mixture of their kind. And we went ahead and did it, you, and you, and I. And now we've sent forth an enemy—safely into the safe hiding place of space, in a ship that can take him across the galaxy, supplied with food to keep him for years, rebuilt into a body that will not die, with star charts and all the keys to understand our culture and locate his home again, using the ability to learn we have encouraged in him."

"I say," said the commander, doggedly, "he is not that dangerous—yet. So far he has done nothing one of us could not do, had we entertained the notion. He's shown nothing, nothing supernormal."

"Hasn't he?" said the doctor thickly. "What about the defensive screen—our most dangerous, most terrible weapon—that could burn him to nothingness if he touched it?"

The commander stared at him.

"But—" said the commander. "The screen was shut off, of course, to let the food carrier out, at the same time the door was opened. I assumed—"

"I checked," said the doctor, his eyes burning on the commander. "They turned it on again before he could get out."

"But he *did* get out! You don't mean . . ." the commander's voice faltered and dropped. The three stood caught in a sudden silence like stone. Slowly, as if drawn by strings controlled by an invisible hand, they turned as one to stare up into the empty sky and space beyond.

"You mean—" the commander's voice tried again, and died.

"Exactly!" whispered the doctor.

Halfway across the galaxy, a child of a sensitive race cried out in its sleep and clutched at its mother.

"I had a bad dream," it whimpered.

"Hush," said its mother. "Hush." But she lay still, staring at the ceiling. She, too, had dreamed.

Somewhere, Eldridge was smiling at the stars.

ALL THE PEOPLE

R. A. Lafferty

How many people do you know? Two hundred? A thousand? Ten thousand? You've probably never tried to make a list, but if you did, most likely you'd be surprised at how long it is. Not so long, though, as the list of Anthony Trotz, who—and this is the sort of idea that only R. A. Lafferty, that whimsical Oklahoma leprechaun, could be expected to have—discovered one day that he knew everybody. Everybody.

Anthony Trotz went first to the politician, Mike Delado.

"How many people do you know, Mr. Delado?"

"Why the question?"

"I am wondering just what amount of detail the mind can hold."

"To a degree I know many. Ten thousand well, thirty thousand by name, probably a hundred thousand by face and to shake hands with."

"And what is the limit?"

"Possibly I am the limit." The politician smiled frostily. "The only limit is time, speed of cognizance, and retention. I am told that the latter lessens with age. I am seventy, and it has not done so with me. Whom I have known I do not forget."

"And with special training could one go beyond you?"

"I doubt if one could—much. For my own training has been quite special. Nobody has been so entirely with the people as I have. I've taken five memory courses in my time, but the tricks of all of them I had already come to on my own. I am a great believer in the commonality of mankind and of near equal inherent ability. Yet there are some, say the one man in fifty, who in degree if not in kind do exceed their fellows in scope and awareness and vitality. I am that one man in fifty, and knowing people is my specialty."

"Could a man who specialized still more—and to the exclusion of other things—know a hundred thousand men well?"

"It is possible. Dimly."

"A quarter of a million?"

"I think not. He might learn that many faces and names, but he would not know the men."

Anthony went next to the philosopher, Gabriel Mindel.

"Mr. Mindel, how many people do you know?"

"How know? *Per se? A se?* Or *In se? Per suam essentiam,* perhaps? Or do you mean *ab alio?* Or to know as *hoc aliquid?* There is a fine difference there. Or do you possibly mean to know *in substantia prima,* or in the sense of comprehensive *noumena?*"

"Somewhere between the latter two. How many persons do you know by name, face, and with a degree of intimacy?"

"I have learned over the years the names of some of my colleagues, possibly a dozen of them. I am now sound on my wife's name, and I seldom stumble over the names of my offspring—never more than momentarily. But you may have come to the wrong man for . . . whatever you have come for. I am notoriously poor at names, faces, and persons. I have even been described (*vox faucibus haesit*) as absentminded."

"Yes, you do have the reputation. But perhaps I have not come to the wrong man in seeking the theory of the thing. What is it that limits the comprehensive capacity of the mind of man? What will it hold? What restricts?"

"The body."

"How is that?"

"The brain, I should say, the material tie. The mind is limited by the brain. It is skull-bound. It can accumulate no more than its cranial capacity, though not one-tenth of that is ordinarily used. An unbodied mind would (in esoteric theory) be unlimited."

"And how in practical theory?"

"If it is practical, a *pragma*, it is a thing and not a theory."

"Then we can have no experience with the unbodied mind, or the possibility of it?"

"We have not discovered any area of contact, but we may entertain the possibility of it. There is no paradox here. One may rationally consider the irrational."

Anthony went next to see the priest.

"How many people do you know?" he asked him.

"I know them all."

"That has to be doubted," said Anthony after a moment.

"I've had twenty different stations. And when you hear five thousand confessions a year for forty years, you by no means know all about people, but you do know all people."

"I do not mean types. I mean persons."

"Oh, I know a dozen or so well, a few thousand somewhat less."

"Would it be possible to know a hundred thousand people, a half million?"

"A mentalist might know that many to recognize; I don't know the limit. But darkened man has a limit set on everything."

"Could a somehow emancipated man know more?"

"The only emancipated man is the corporeally dead man. And the dead man, if he attains the beatific vision, knows all other persons who have ever been since time began."

"All the billions?"

"All."

"With the same brain?"

"No. But with the same mind."

"Then wouldn't even a believer have to admit that the mind which we have now is only a token mind? Would not any connection it would have with a completely comprehensive mind be very tenuous? Would we really be the same person if so changed? It is like saying a bucket would hold the ocean if it were fulfilled, which only means filled full. How could it be the same mind?"

"I don't know."

Anthony went to see the psychologist.

"How many people do you know, Dr. Shirm?"

"I could be crabby and say that I know as many as I want to; but it wouldn't be the truth. I rather like people, which is odd in my profession. What is it that you really want to know?"

"How many people can one man know?"

"It doesn't matter very much. People mostly overestimate the number of their acquaintances. What is it that you are trying to ask me?"

"Could one man know everyone?"

"Naturally not. But unnaturally he might seem to. There is a delusion to this effect accompanied by euphoria, and it is called—"

"I don't want to know what it is called. Why do specialists use Latin and Greek?"

"One part hokum, and two parts need; there simply not being enough letters in the alphabet of exposition without them. It is as difficult to name concepts as children, and we search our brains as a new mother does. It will not do to call two children or two concepts by the same name."

"Thank you. I doubt that this is delusion, and it is not accompanied by euphoria."

Anthony had a reason for questioning the four men since (as a new thing that had come to him) he knew everybody. He knew everyone in Salt Lake City, where he had never been. He knew everybody in Jebel Shah, where the town is a little amphitheater around the harbor, and in Batangas and Weihai. He knew the loungers around the end of the Galata bridge in Istanbul, and the porters in Kuala Lumpur. He knew the tobacco traders in Plovdiv, and the cork cutters of Portugal. He knew the dock workers in Djibouti, and the glove makers in Prague. He knew the vegetable farmers around El Centro, and the muskrat trappers of Barataria Bay. He knew the three billion people of the world by name and face, and with a fair degree of intimacy.

"Yet I'm not a very intelligent man. I've been called a bungler. And they've had to reassign me three different times at the filter center. I've seen only a few thousands of those billions of people, and it seems unusual that I should know them all. It may be a delusion, as Dr. Shirm says, but it is a heavily detailed delusion, and it is not accompanied by euphoria. I feel like green hell just thinking of it."

He knew the cattle traders of Letterkenny, Donegal; he knew the cane cutters of Oriente, and the tree climbers of Milne Bay. He knew the people who died every minute, and those who were born.

"There is no way out of it. I know everybody in the world. It is impossible, but it is so. And to what purpose? There aren't a handful of them I could borrow a dollar from, and I haven't a real friend in the lot. I don't know whether it came to me suddenly, but I realized it suddenly. My father was a junk dealer in Wichita, and my education is spotty. I am maladjusted, introverted, incompetent and unhappy, and I also have weak kidneys. Why should a power like this come to a man like me?"

The children in the streets hooted at him. Anthony had always had a healthy hatred for children and dogs, those twin harassers of the unfortunate and the maladjusted. Both run in packs, and both are cowardly attackers. If either of them spots a weakness he will never let it go. That Anthony's father had been a junk dealer was no reason to hoot at him. And how did the children even know about that? Did they possess some fraction of the power that had come on him lately?

But he had strolled about the town for too long. He should have been at work at the filter center. Often they were impatient with him when he wandered off from his work, and Colonel Peter Cooper was waiting for him when he came in now.

"Where have you been, Anthony?"

"Walking. I talked to four men. I mentioned no subject in the province of the filter center."

"Every subject is in the province of the filter center. And you know that our work here is confidential."

"Yes, sir, but I do not understand the import of my work here. I would not be able to give out information that I do not have."

"A popular misconception. There are others who might understand the import of it, and be able to reconstruct it from what you tell them. How do you feel?"

"Nervous, unwell, my tongue is furred, and my kidneys—"

"Ah yes, there will be someone here this afternoon to fix your kidneys. I have not forgotten. Is there anything that you want to tell me?"

"No, sir."

Colonel Cooper had the habit of asking that of his workers in the manner of a mother asking a child if he wants to go to the bathroom. There was something embarrassing in his intonation.

Well, he did want to tell him something, but he didn't know how to phrase it. He wanted to tell the Colonel that he had newly acquired the power of knowing everyone in the world, that he was worried how he could hold so much in a head that was not noteworthy for its capacity. But he feared ridicule more than he feared anything and he was a tangle of fears.

But he thought he would try it a little bit on his co-workers.

"I know a man named Walter Walloroy in Galveston," he said to Adrian. "He drinks beer at the Gizmo bar, and is retired."

"What is the superlative of *so what?*"

"But I have never been there," said Anthony.

"And I have never been in Kalamazoo."

"I know a girl in Kalamazoo. Her name is Greta Harandash. She is home today with a cold. She is prone to colds."

But Adrian was a creature both uninterested and uninteresting. It is very hard to confide in one who is uninterested.

"Well, I will live with it a little while," said Anthony. "Or I may have to go to a doctor and see if he can give me something to make all these people go away. But if he thinks my story is a queer one, he may report me back to the center, and I might be reclassified again. It makes me nervous to be reclassified."

So he lived with it a while, the rest of the day and the night. He should have felt better. A man had come that afternoon and fixed his kidneys; but there was nobody to fix his nervousness and apprehension. And his skittishness was increased when the children hooted at him as he walked to work in the morning. That hated epithet! But how could they know that his father had been a dealer in used metals in a town far away?

He had to confide in someone.

He spoke to Wellington, who also worked in his room. "I know a girl in Beirut who is just going to bed. It is evening there now, you know."

"That so? Why don't they get their time straightened out? I met a girl last night that's cute as a correlator key, and kind of shaped like one. She doesn't know yet that I work in the center and am a restricted person. I'm not going to tell her. Let her find out for herself."

It was no good trying to tell things to Wellington. Wellington never listened. And then Anthony got a summons to Colonel Peter Cooper, which always increased his apprehension.

"Anthony," said the Colonel, "I want you to tell me if you discern anything unusual. That is really your job, to report anything unusual. The other, the paper shuffling, is just something to keep your idle hands busy. Now tell me clearly if anything unusual has come to your notice."

"Sir, it has." And then he blurted it out. "I know everybody. I know everybody in the world. I know them all in their billions, every person. It has me worried sick."

"Yes, yes, Anthony. But tell me, have you noticed anything *odd*? It is your duty to tell me if you have."

"But I have just told you! In some manner I know every person in the world. I know the people in Transvaal, I know the people in Guatemala. I know *everybody*."

"Yes, Anthony, we realize that. And it may take a little getting used to. But that isn't what I mean. Have you, besides that thing that seems out of the way to you, noticed anything unusual, anything that seems out of place, a little bit wrong?"

"Ah, besides that and your reaction to it, no, sir. Nothing else odd. I might ask, though, how odd can a thing get? But other than that, no, sir."

"Good, Anthony. Now remember, if you sense anything odd

about anything at all, come and tell me. No matter how trivial it is, if you feel that something is just a little bit out of place, then report it at once. Do you understand that?"

"Yes, sir."

But he couldn't help wondering what it might be that the Colonel would consider a little bit odd.

Anthony left the center and walked. He shouldn't have. He knew that they became impatient with him when he wandered off from his work.

"But I have to think. I have all the people in the world in my brain, and still I am not able to think. This power should have come to someone able to take advantage of it."

He went into the Plugged Nickel Bar, but the man on duty knew him for a restricted person from the filter center, and would not serve him.

He wandered disconsolately about the city. "I know the people in Omaha and those in Omsk. What queer names have the towns of the earth! I know everyone in the world, and when anyone is born or dies. And Colonel Cooper did not find it unusual. Yet I am to be on the lookout for things unusual. The question rises, would I know an odd thing if I met it?"

And then it was that something just a little bit unusual did happen, something not quite right, a small thing. But the Colonel had told him to report anything about anything, no matter how insignificant, that struck him as a little queer.

It was just that with all the people in his head, and the arrivals and departures, there was a small group that was not of the pattern. Every minute hundreds left by death and arrived by birth. And now there was a small group, seven persons; they arrived into the world, and they were not born into the world.

So Anthony went to tell Colonel Cooper that something had occurred to his mind that was a little bit odd.

But damn-the-dander-headed-two-and-four-legged devils, there were the kids and the dogs in the street again, yipping and hooting and chanting:

"Tony the tin man, Tony the tin man."

He longed for the day when he would see them fall like leaves out of his mind, and death take them.

"Tony the tin man, Tony the tin man."

How had they known that his father was a used-metal dealer?

Colonel Peter Cooper was waiting for him.

"You surely took your time, Anthony. Tell me at once what it is and where. The reaction was registered, but it would take us hours to pinpoint its source without your help. Now then, explain as calmly as you can what you felt or experienced. Or, more to the point, where are they?"

"No. You will have to answer certain questions first."

"I haven't the time to waste, Anthony. Tell me at once what it is and where."

"No. There is no other way. You have to bargain with me."

"One does not bargain with restricted persons."

"Well, I will bargain till I find out just what it means that I am a restricted person."

"You really don't know? Well, we haven't time to fix that stubborn streak in you now. Quickly, just what is it that you have to know?"

"I have to know what a restricted person is. I have to know why the children hoot 'Tony the tin man' at me. How can they know that my father was a junk dealer?"

"You had no father. We give to each of you a basic collection of concepts and the vocabulary to handle them, a sufficient store of memories, and a background of a distant town. That happened to be yours, but there is no connection here. The children call you Tony the Tin Man because, like all really cruel creatures, they have an instinct for the truth that can hurt; and they will never forget it."

"Then I am a tin man?"

"Well, no. Actually only seventeen percent metal. And less than a third of one percent tin. You are compounded of animal, vegetable, and mineral fiber, and there was much effort given to your manufacture and programming. Yet the taunt of the children is essentially true."

"Then, if I am Tony the Tin Man, how can I know all the people of the world in my mind?"

"You have no mind."

"In my brain then. How can all that be in one small brain?"

"Because your brain is not in your head, and it is not small. The longest way around may take the shortest time here. Come, I may as well show it to you. I've told you enough that it won't matter if you know a little more. There are few who are taken on personally conducted sightseeing tours of their own brains. You should be grateful."

"Gratitude seems a little tardy."

They went into the barred area, down into the bowels of the main building of the center. And they looked at the brain of Anthony Trotz, a restricted person in its special meaning.

"It is the largest in the world," said Colonel Cooper.

"How large?"

"A little over twelve hundred cubic meters."

"What a brain! And it is mine?"

"You share it with others. But, yes, it is yours. You have access to its data. You are an adjunct to it, a runner for it, an appendage, inasmuch as you are anything at all."

"Colonel Cooper, how long have I been alive?"

"You are not."

"How long have I been as I am now?"

"It is three days since you were last reassigned, since you were assigned to this. At that time your nervousness and apprehensions were introduced. An apprehensive unit will be more inclined to notice details just a little out of the ordinary."

"And what is my purpose?"

They were now walking back to the office work area, and Anthony had a sad feeling at leaving his brain behind him.

"This is a filter center," said Colonel Cooper, "and your purpose is to serve as a filter, of a sort. Every person has a slight aura about him. It is a characteristic of his, and is part of his personality and purpose. And it can be detected, electrically, magnetically, even visually under special conditions. The accumulator at which we were looking (your brain) is designed to maintain contact with all the auras in the world, and to keep running and complete data on them all. It contains a multiplicity of circuits for each of its three-billion-and-some subjects. However, as aid to its operation, it was necessary to assign several artificial consciousnesses to it. You are one of these."

Anthony looked out the window as the Colonel continued his explanation.

The dogs and the children had found a new victim in the streets below, and Anthony's heart went out to him.

"The purpose," said Colonel Cooper, "was to notice anything just a little peculiar in the auras and the persons they represent, anything at all odd in their comings and goings. Anything like what you have come here to report to me."

"Like the seven persons who recently arrived in the world, and not by way of birth?"

"Yes. We have been expecting the first of the aliens for months. We must know their area, and at once. Now tell me."

"What if they are not aliens at all? What if they are restricted persons like myself?"

"Restricted persons have no aura, are not persons, are not alive. And you would not receive knowledge of them."

"Then how do I know the other restricted persons here, Adrian and Wellington, and such?"

"You know them at first hand. You do not know them through the machine. Now tell me the area quickly. The center may be a primary target. It will take the machine hours to ravel it out. Your only purpose is to serve as an intuitive shortcut."

But Tin Man Tony did not speak. He only thought in his mind —more accurately, in his brain a hundred yards away. He thought in his fabricated consciousness:

The area is quite near. If the Colonel were not burdened with a mind, he would be able to think more clearly. He would know that cruel children and dogs love to worry what is not human, and that all the restricted persons for this area are accounted for. He would know that they are worrying one of the aliens in the street below, and that is the area that is right for my consciousness.

I wonder if they will be better masters? He is an imposing figure, and he would be able to pass for a man. And the Colonel is right: the center is a primary target.

Why! I never knew you could kill a child just by pointing a finger at him like that! What opportunities I have missed! Enemy of my enemy, you are my friend.

And aloud he said to the Colonel:

"I will not tell you."

"Then we'll have you apart and get it out of you mighty quick."

"How quick?"

"Ten minutes."

"Time enough," said Tony.

For he knew them now, coming in like snow. They were arriving in the world by the hundreds, and not arriving by birth.

ODDY AND ID

Alfred Bester

Insurance-company claims adjusters are all too familiar with the concept of the accident-prone person: someone to whom awful things happen regularly, not through carelessness or stupidity so much as through sheer ghastly luck. In this crisp little story Alfred Bester, author of those classic novels The Demolished Man *and* The Stars My Destination, *turns that concept upside down to examine the glittering career of Odysseus Gaul, who was fortune-prone, who had the gift of eternal good luck.*

This is the story of a monster.

They named him Odysseus Gaul in honor of Papa's favorite hero, and over Mama's desperate objections; but he was known as Oddy from the age of one.

The first year of life is an egotistic craving for warmth and security. Oddy was not likely to have much of that when he was born, for Papa's real-estate business was bankrupt, and Mama was thinking of divorce. But an unexpected decision by United Radiation to build a plant in the town made Papa wealthy, and Mama fell in love with him all over again. So Oddy had warmth and security.

The second year of life is a timid exploration. Oddy crawled and explored. When he reached for the crimson coils inside the nonobjective fireplace, an unexpected short circuit saved him from a burn. When he fell out of the third-floor window, it was into the grass-filled hopper of the Mechano-Gardener. When he teased the Phoebus Cat, it slipped as it snapped at his face, and the brilliant fangs clicked harmlessly over his ear.

"Animals love Oddy," Mama said. "They only pretend to bite."

Oddy wanted to be loved, so everybody loved Oddy. He was petted, pampered and spoiled through pre-school age. Shopkeepers presented him with largess, and acquaintances showered him with gifts. Of sodas, candy, tarts, chrystons, bobble-trucks, freezies, and various other comestibles, Oddy consumed enough for an entire kindergarten. He was never sick.

"Takes after his father," Papa said. "Good stock."

Family legends grew about Oddy's luck. . . . How a perfect stranger mistook him for his own child just as Oddy was about to amble into the Electronic Circus, and delayed him long enough to save him from the disastrous explosion of '98. . . . How a forgotten library book rescued him from the Rocket Crash of '99. . . . How a multitude of odd incidents saved him from a multitude of assorted catastrophes. No one realized he was a monster . . . yet.

At eighteen, he was a nice-looking boy with seal-brown hair, warm brown eyes, and a wide grin that showed even, white teeth. He was strong, healthy, intelligent. He was completely uninhibited in his quiet, relaxed way. He had charm. He was happy. So far, his monstrous evil had only affected the little Town Unit where he was born and raised.

He came to Harvard from a progressive school, so when one of his many new friends popped into the dormitory room and said, "Hey, Oddy, come down to the Quad and kick a ball around," Oddy answered: "I don't know how, Ben."

"Don't know how?" Ben tucked the football under his arm and dragged Oddy with him. "Where you been, laddie?"

"They didn't think much of football back home," Oddy

grinned. "Said it was old-fashioned. We were strictly Huxley-Hob."

"Huxley-Hob! That's for eggheads," Ben said. "Football is still the big game. You want to be famous? You got to be on that gridiron on TV every Saturday."

"So I've noticed, Ben. Show me."

Ben showed Oddy, carefully and with patience. Oddy took the lesson seriously and industriously. His third punt was caught by a freakish gust of wind, traveled seventy yards through the air, and burst through the third-floor window of Proctor Charley (Gravy-Train) Stuart. Stuart took one look out the window and had Oddy down to Soldier Stadium in half an hour. Three Saturdays later, the headlines read: Oddy Gaul 57–Army 0.

"Snell and rumination!" Coach Hig Clayton swore. "How does he do it? There's nothing sensational about that kid. He's just average. But when he runs, they fall down chasing him. When he kicks, they fumble. When they fumble, he recovers."

"He's a negative player," Gravy-Train answered. "He lets you make the mistakes and then he cashes in."

They were both wrong. Oddy Gaul was a monster.

With his choice of any eligible young woman, Oddy Gaul went stag to the Observatory Prom, wandered into a darkroom by mistake, and discovered a girl in a smock bending over trays in the hideous green safe-light. She had cropped black hair, icy-blue eyes, strong features, and a sensuous boyish figure. She ordered him out and Oddy fell in love with her . . . temporarily.

His friends howled with laughter when he told them. "Shades of Pygmalion, Oddy, don't you know about *her*? The girl is frigid. A statue. She loathes men. You're wasting your time."

But through the adroitness of her analyst, the girl turned a neurotic corner one week later and fell deeply in love with Oddy Gaul. It was sudden, devastating, and enraptured for two months. Then just as Oddy began to cool, the girl had a relapse and everything ended on a friendly, convenient basis.

So far only minor events had made up the response to Oddy's luck, but the shock-wave of reaction was spreading. In September of his sophomore year, Oddy competed for the Political Economy

Medal with a thesis entitled: "Causes of Mutiny." The striking similarity of his paper to the Astraean Mutiny that broke out the day his paper was entered won him the prize.

In October, Oddy contributed twenty-five dollars to a pool organized by a crack-pot classmate for speculating on the Exchange according to "Stock Market Trends," an ancient superstition. The prophet's calculations were ridiculous, but a sharp panic nearly ruined the Exchange as it quadrupled the pool. Oddy made one hundred dollars.

And so it went . . . worse and worse. The monster.

Now a monster can get away with a lot when he's studying a speculative philosophy where causation is rooted in history and the Present is devoted to statistical analysis of the Past; but the living sciences are bulldogs with their teeth clamped on the phenomena of Now. So it was Jesse Migg, physiologist and spectral physicist, who first trapped the monster . . . and he thought he'd found an angel.

Old Jess was one of the Sights. In the first place he was young . . . not over forty. He was a malignant knife of a man, an albino, pink-eyed, bald, pointed-nosed and brilliant. He affected twentieth-century clothes and twentieth-century vices . . . tobacco and potations of C_2H_5OH. He never talked. . . . He spat. He never walked. . . . He scurried. And he was scurrying up and down the aisles of the laboratory of Tech I (General Survey of Spatial Mechanics—Required for All General Arts Students) when he ferreted out the monster.

One of the first experiments in the course was EMF Electrolysis. Elementary stuff. A U-tube containing water was passed between the poles of a stock Remosant magnet. After sufficient voltage had been transmitted through the coils, you drew off hydrogen and oxygen in two-to-one ratio at the arms of the tube and related them to the voltage and the magnetic field.

Oddy ran his experiment earnestly, got the approved results, entered them in his lab book and then waited for the official check-off. Little Migg came hustling down the aisle, darted to Oddy and spat: "Finished?"

"Yes, sir."

Migg checked the book entries, glanced at the indicators at the ends of the tube, and stamped Oddy out with a sneer. It was only after Oddy was gone that he noticed the Remosant magnet was obviously shorted. The wires were fused. There hadn't been any field to electrolyze the water.

"Hell and damnation!" Migg grunted (he also affected twentieth-century vituperation) and rolled a clumsy cigarette.

He checked off possibilities in his comptometer head. 1. Gaul cheated. 2. If so, with what apparatus did he portion out the H_2 and O_2? 3. Where did he get the pure gases? 4. Why did he do it? Honesty was easier. 5. He didn't cheat. 6. How did he get the right results? 7. How did he get *any* results?

Old Jess emptied the U-tube, refilled it with water and ran off the experiment himself. He too got the correct result without a magnet.

"Christ on a raft!" he swore, unimpressed by the miracle, and infuriated by the mystery. He snooped, darting about like a hungry bat. After four hours he discovered that the steel bench supports were picking up a charge from the Greeson coils in the basement and had thrown just enough field to make everything come out right.

"Coincidence," Migg spat. But he was not convinced.

Two weeks later, in Elementary Fission Analysis, Oddy completed his afternoon's work with a careful listing of resultant isotopes from selenium to lanthanum. The only trouble, Migg discovered, was that there had been a mistake in the stock issued to Oddy. He hadn't received any U^{235} for neutron bombardment. His sample had been a leftover from a Stefan-Boltsmann blackbody demonstration.

"God in Heaven!" Migg swore, and double-checked. Then he triple-checked. When he found the answer—a remarkable coincidence involving improperly cleaned apparatus and a defective cloud chamber—he swore further. He also did some intensive thinking.

"There are accident prones," Migg snarled at the reflection in his Self-Analysis Mirror. "How about good-luck prones? Horse manure!"

But he was a bulldog with his teeth sunk in phenomena. He tested Oddy Gaul. He hovered over him in the laboratory, cackling with infuriated glee as Oddy completed experiment after experiment with defective equipment. When Oddy successfully completed the Rutherford Classic—getting $_8O^{17}$ after exposing nitrogen to alpha radiation, but in this case without the use of nitrogen or alpha radiation—Migg actually clapped him on the back in delight. Then the little man investigated and found the logical, improbable chain of coincidences that explained it.

He devoted his spare time to a check-back on Oddy's career at Harvard. He had a two-hour conference with a lady astronomer's faculty analyst, and a ten-minute talk with Hig Clayton and Gravy-Train Stuart. He rooted out the Exchange Pool, the Political Economy Medal, and half a dozen other incidents that filled him with malignant joy. Then he cast off his twentieth-century affectation, dressed himself properly in formal leotards, and entered the Faculty Club for the first time in a year.

A four-handed chess game on a transparent toroid board was in progress in the Diathermy Alcove. It had been in progress since Migg joined the faculty, and would probably not be finished before the end of the century. In fact, Johansen, playing Red, was already training his son to replace him in the likely event of his dying before the completion of the game.

As abrupt as ever, Migg marched up to the glowing board, sparkling with vari-colored pieces, and blurted: "What do you know about accidents?"

"Ah?" said Bellanby, *Philosopher in Res* at the University. "Good evening, Migg. Do you mean the accident of substance, or the accident of essence? If, on the other hand, your question implies—"

"No, no," Migg interrupted. "My apologies, Bellanby. Let me rephrase the question. Is there such a thing as compulsion of probability?"

Hrrdnikkisch completed his move and gave full attention to Migg, as did Johansen and Bellanby. Wilson continued to study the board. Since he was permitted one hour to make his move and would need it, Migg knew there would be ample time for the discussion.

"Compulsion of probability?" Hrrdnikkisch lisped. "Not a new concept, Migg. I recall a thurvey of the theme in 'The Integraph,' Volume LVIII, Number 9. The calculuth, if I am not mithtaken—"

"No," Migg interrupted again. "My respects, Signoid. I'm not interested in the mathematic of probability, nor the philosophy. Let me put it this way. The accident-prone has already been incorporated into the body of psychoanalysis. Paton's Theorem of the Least Neurotic Norm settled that. But I've discovered the obverse. I've discovered a fortune-prone."

"Ah?" Johansen chuckled. "It's to be a joke. You wait and see, Signoid."

"No," answered Migg. "I'm perfectly serious. I've discovered a genuinely lucky man."

"He wins at cards?"

"He wins at everything. Accept this postulate for the moment. . . . I'll document it later. . . . There is a man who is lucky. He is a fortune-prone. Whatever he desires, he receives. Whether he has the ability to achieve it or not, he receives it. If his desire is totally beyond the peak of his accomplishment, then the factors of chance, coincidence, hazard, accident . . . and so on, combine to produce his desired end."

"No." Bellanby shook his head. "Too far-fetched."

"I've worked it out empirically," Migg continued. "It's something like this. The future is a choice of mutually exclusive possibilities, one or other of which must be realized in terms of favorability of the events and number of the events. . . ."

"Yes, yes," interrupted Johansen. "The greater the number of favorable possibilities, the stronger the probability of an event maturing. This is elementary, Migg. Go on."

"I continue," Migg spat indignantly. "When we discuss probability in terms of throwing dice, the predictions or odds are simple. There are only six mutually exclusive possibilities to each die. The favorability is easy to compute. Chance is reduced to simple odds-ratios. *But* when we discuss probability in terms of the Universe, we cannot encompass enough data to make a prediction.

There are too many factors. Favorability cannot be ascertained."

"All thith ith true," Hrrdnikkisch said, "but what of your fortune-prone?"

"I can't know how he does it . . . but merely by the intensity or mere existence of his desire, he can affect the favorability of possibilities. By wanting, he can turn possibility into probability, and probability into certainty."

"Ridiculous," Bellanby snapped. "You claim there's a man far-sighted and far-reaching enough to do this?"

"Nothing of the sort. He doesn't know what he's doing. He just thinks he's lucky, if he thinks about it at all. Let us say he wants . . . oh . . . name anything."

"Heroin," Bellanby said.

"What's that?" Johansen inquired.

"A morphine derivative," Hrrdnikkisch explained. "Formerly manufactured and thold to narcotic addictth."

"Heroin," Migg said. "Excellent. Say my man desires heroin, an antique narcotic no longer in existence. Very good. His desire would compel this sequence of possible but improbable events: A chemist in Australia, fumbling through a new organic synthesis, will accidentally and unwittingly prepare six ounces of heroin. Four ounces will be discarded, but through a logical mistake two ounces will be preserved. A further coincidence will ship it to this country and this city, wrapped as powdered sugar in a plastic ball; where the final accident will serve it to my man in a restaurant which he is visiting for the first time on an impulse. . . ."

"La-la-la!" said Hrrdnikkisch. "Thith shuffling of hithtory. Thith fluctuation of inthident and pothibility? All achieved without the knowledge but with the dethire of a man?"

"Yes. Precisely my point," Migg snarled. "I don't know how he does it, but he turns possibility into certainty. And since almost anything is possible, he is capable of accomplishing almost anything. He is godlike but not a god because he does this without consciousness. He is an angel."

"Who is this angel?" Johansen asked.

And Migg told them all about Oddy Gaul.

"But how does he do it?" Bellanby persisted. "How does he do it?"

"I don't know," Migg repeated again. "Tell me how Espers do it."

"What!" Bellanby exclaimed. "Are you prepared to deny the telepathic pattern of thought? Do you–"

"I do nothing of the sort. I merely illustrate one possible explanation. Man produces events. The threatening War of Resources may be thought to be a result of the natural exhaustion of Terran resources. We know it is not. It is a result of centuries of thriftless waste by man. Natural phenomena are less often produced by nature and more often produced by man."

"And?"

"Who knows? Gaul is producing phenomena. Perhaps he's unconsciously broadcasting on a telepathic wave band. Broadcasting and getting results. He wants heroin. The broadcast goes out–"

"But Espers can't pick up any telepathic pattern further than the horizon. It's direct-wave transmission. Even large objects cannot be penetrated. A building, say, or a–"

"I'm not saying this is on the Esper level," Migg shouted. "I'm trying to imagine something bigger. Something tremendous. He wants heroin. His broadcast goes out to the world. All men unconsciously fall into a pattern of activity which will produce that heroin as quickly as possible. That Austrian chemist–"

"No, Australian."

"That Australian chemist may have been debating between half a dozen different syntheses. Five of them could never have produced heroin; but Gaul's impulse made him select the sixth."

"And if he did not anyway?"

"Then who knows what parallel chains were also started? A boy playing Robin Hood in Montreal is impelled to explore an abandoned cabin where he finds the drug, hidden there centuries ago by smugglers. A woman in California collects old apothecary jars. She finds a pound of heroin. A child in Berlin, playing with a defective Radar-Chem Set, manufactures it. Name the most improbable sequence of events, and Gaul can bring it about, logically and certainly. I tell you, that boy is an angel!"

And he produced his documented evidence and convinced them.

It was then that four scholars of various but indisputable intellects elected themselves an executive committee for Fate and took Oddy Gaul in hand. To understand what they attempted to do, you must first understand the situation the world found itself in during that particular era.

It is a known fact that all wars are founded in economic conflict, or to put it another way, a trial by arms is merely the last battle of an economic war. In the pre-Christian centuries, the Punic Wars were the final outcome of a financial struggle between Rome and Carthage for economic control of the Mediterranean. Three thousand years later, the impending War of Resources loomed as the finale of a struggle between the two Independent Welfare States controlling most of the known economic world.

What petroleum oil was to the twentieth century, FO (the nickname for Fissionable Ore) was to the thirtieth; and the situation was peculiarly similar to the Asia Minor crisis that ultimately wrecked the United Nations a thousand years before. Triton, a backward semibarbaric satellite, previously unwanted and ignored, had suddenly discovered it possessed enormous resources of FO. Financially and technologically incapable of self-development, Triton was peddling concessions to both Welfare States.

The difference between a Welfare State and a Benevolent Despot is slight. In times of crisis, either can be traduced by the sincerest motives into the most abominable conduct. Both the Comity of Nations (bitterly nicknamed "The Con Men" by Der Realpolitik aus Terra) and Der Realpolitik aus Terra (sardonically called "The Rats" by the Comity of Nations) were desperately in need of natural resources, meaning FO. They were bidding against each other hysterically, and elbowing each other with sharp skirmishes at outposts. Their sole concern was the protection of their citizens. From the best of motives they were preparing to cut each other's throats.

Had this been the issue before the citizens of both Welfare States, some compromise might have been reached; but Triton, intoxicated as a schoolboy with a newfound prominence and power, confused issues by raising a religious issue and reviving a Holy War which the Family of Planets had long forgotten. Assistance in their Holy War (involving the extermination of a harmless and rather unimportant sect called the Quakers) was one of the conditions of sale. This, both the Comity of Nations and Der Realpolitik aus Terra were prepared to swallow with or without private reservations, but it could not be admitted to their citizens.

And so, camouflaged by the burning issues of Rights of Minority Sects, Priority of Pioneering, Freedom of Religion, Historical Rights to Triton v. Possession in Fact, etc., the two Houses of the Family of Planets feinted, parried, riposted and slowly closed, like fencers on the strip, for the final sortie which meant ruin for both.

All this the four men discussed through three interminable meetings.

"Look here," Migg complained toward the close of the third consultation. "You theoreticians have already turned nine man-hours into carbonic acid with ridiculous dissensions . . ."

Bellanby nodded, smiling. "It's as I've always said, Migg. Every man nurses the secret belief that were he God he could do the job much better. We're just learning how difficult it is."

"Not God," Hrrdnikkisch said, "but hith Prime Minithterth. Gaul will be God."

Johansen winced. "I don't like that talk," he said. "I happen to be a religious man."

"You?" Bellanby exclaimed in surprise. "A Colloid-Therapeutist?"

"I happen to be a religious man," Johansen repeated stubbornly.

"But the boy hath the power of the miracle," Hrrdnikkisch protested. "When he hath been taught to know what he doth, he will be a God."

"This is pointless," Migg rapped out. "We have spent three sessions in piffling discussion. I have heard three opposed views re Mr. Odysseus Gaul. Although all are agreed he must be used as a tool, none can agree on the work to which the tool must be set. Bellanby prattles about an Ideal Intellectual Anarchy, Johansen preaches about a Soviet of God, and Hrrdnikkisch has wasted two hours postulating and destroying his own theorems. . . ."

"Really, Migg . . ." Hrrdnikkisch began. Migg waved his hand.

"Permit me," Migg continued malevolently, "to reduce this discussion to the kindergarten level. First things first, gentlemen. Before attempting to reach cosmic agreement we must make sure there is a cosmos left for us to agree upon. I refer to the impending war. . . .

"Our program, as I see it, must be simple and direct. It is the education of a God or, if Johansen protests, of an angel. Fortunately Gaul is an estimable young man of kindly, honest disposition. I shudder to think what he might have done had he been inherently vicious."

"Or what he might do once he learns what he can do," muttered Bellanby.

"Precisely. We must begin a careful and rigorous ethical education of the boy, but we haven't enough time. We can't educate first, and then explain the truth when he's safe. We must forestall the war. We need a shortcut."

"All right," Johansen said. "What do you suggest?"

"Dazzlement," Migg spat. "Enchantment."

"Enchantment?" Hrrdnikkisch chuckled. "A new thienthe, Migg?"

"Why do you think I selected you three of all people for this secret?" Migg snorted. "For your intellects? Nonsense! I can think you all under the table. No. I selected you, gentlemen, for your charm."

"It's an insult," Bellanby grinned, "and yet I'm flattered."

"Gaul is nineteen," Migg went on. "He is at the age when undergraduates are most susceptible to hero worship. I want you gentlemen to charm him. You are not the first brains of the University, but you are the first heroes."

"I altho am inthulted and flattered," said Hrrdnikkisch.

"I want you to charm him, dazzle him, inspire him with affection and awe . . . as you've done with countless classes of undergraduates."

"Aha!" said Johansen. "The chocolate around the pill."

"Exactly. When he's enchanted, you will make him want to stop the war . . . and then tell him how he can stop it. That will give us breathing space to continue his education. By the time he outgrows his respect for you he will have a sound ethical foundation on which to build. He'll be safe."

"And you, Migg?" Bellanby inquired. "What part do you play?"

"Now? None," Migg snarled. "I have no charm, gentlemen. I come later. When he outgrows his respect for you, he'll begin to acquire respect for me."

All of which was frightfully conceited but perfectly true.

And as events slowly marched toward the final crisis, Oddy Gaul was carefully and quickly enchanted. Bellanby invited him to the twenty-foot crystal globe atop his house . . . the famous hen-roost to which only the favored few were invited. There, Oddy Gaul sun-bathed and admired the philosopher's magnificent iron-hard condition at seventy-three. Admiring Bellanby's muscles, it was only natural for him to admire Bellanby's ideas. He returned often to sun-bathe, worship the great man, and absorb ethical concepts.

Meanwhile, Hrrdnikkisch took over Oddy's evenings. With the mathematician, who puffed and lisped like some flamboyant character out of Rabelais, Oddy was carried to the dizzy heights of the haute cuisine and the complete pagan life. Together they ate and drank incredible foods and liquids and pursued incredible women until Oddy returned to his room each night intoxicated with the magic of the senses and the riotous color of the great Hrrdnikkisch's glittering ideas.

And occasionally . . . not too often, he would find Papa Johansen waiting for him, and then would come the long, quiet talks through the small hours when young men search for the harmonics of life and the meaning of entity. And there was Johansen for Oddy to model himself after . . . a glowing embodiment of Spiritual Good . . . a living example of Faith in God and Ethical Sanity.

The climax came on March 15 . . . the Ides of March, and they should have taken the date as a sign. After dinner with his three heroes at the Faculty Club, Oddy was ushered into the Foto-Library by the three great men where they were joined, quite casually, by Jesse Migg. There passed a few moments of uneasy tension until Migg made a sign, and Bellanby began.

"Oddy," he said, "have you ever had the fantasy that some day you might wake up and discover you were a king?"

Oddy blushed.

"I see you have. You know, every man has entertained that dream. It's called the Mignon Complex. The usual pattern is: You learn your parents have only adopted you, and that you are actually and rightfully the king of . . . of . . ."

"Barataria," said Hrrdnikkisch, who had made a study of Stone Age Fiction.

"Yes, sir," Oddy muttered. "I've had that dream."

"Well," Bellanby said quietly, "it's come true. You are a King."

Oddy stared while they explained and explained and explained. First, as a college boy, he was wary and suspicious of a joke. Then, as an idolator, he was almost persuaded by the men he most admired. And finally, as a human animal, he was swept away by the exaltation of security. Not power, not glory, not wealth thrilled him, but security alone. Later he might come to enjoy the trimmings, but now he was released from fear. He need never worry again.

"Yes," exclaimed Oddy. "Yes, yes, yes! I understand. I understand what you want me to do." He surged up excitedly from his chair and circled the illuminated walls, trembling with joy. Then he stopped and turned.

"And I'm grateful," he said. "Grateful to all of you for what you've been trying to do. It would have been shameful if I'd been selfish . . . or mean. . . . Trying to use this for myself. But you've shown me the way. It's to be used for good. Always!"

Johansen nodded happily.

"I'll always listen to you," Oddy went on. "I don't want to make any mistakes. Ever!" He paused and blushed again. "That dream about being a king . . . I had that when I was a kid. But here at the school I've had something bigger. I used to wonder what would happen if I was the one man who could run the world. I used to dream about the kind, generous things I'd do. . . ."

"Yes," said Bellanby. "We know, Oddy. We've all had that dream too. Every man does."

"But it isn't a dream any more," Oddy laughed. "It's reality. I can do it. I can make it happen."

"Start with the war," Migg said sourly.

"Of course," said Oddy. "The war first; but then we'll go on from there, won't we? I'll make sure the war never starts, but then we'll do big things . . . great things! Just the five of us in private. Nobody'll know about us. We'll be ordinary people, but we'll make life wonderful for everybody. If I'm an angel . . . like you say . . . then I'll spread heaven around me as far as I can reach."

"But start with the war," Migg repeated.

"The war is the first disaster that must be averted, Oddy," Bellanby said. "If you don't want this disaster to happen, it will never happen."

"And you want to prevent that tragedy, don't you?" said Johansen.

"Yes," answered Oddy. "I do."

On March 20, the war broke. The Comity of Nations and Der Realpolitik aus Terra mobilized and struck. While blow followed shattering counterblow, Oddy Gaul was commissioned subaltern in a line regiment, but gazetted to Intelligence on May 3. On June 24 he was appointed A.D.C. to the Joint Forces Council meeting in the ruins of what had been Australia. On July 11, he was brevetted to command of the wrecked Space Force, being jumped 1,789 grades over regular officers. On September 19 he assumed supreme command in the Battle of the Parsec and won the victory that ended the disastrous solar annihilation called the Six Months' War.

On September 23, Oddy Gaul made the astonishing peace offer that was accepted by the remnants of both Welfare States. It required the scrapping of antagonistic economic theories, and amounted to the virtual abandonment of all economic theory with an amalgamation of both States into a Solar Society. On January 1, Oddy Gaul, by unanimous acclaim, was elected Solon of the Solar Society in perpetuity.

And today . . . still youthful, still vigorous, still handsome, still sincere, idealistic, charitable, kindly and sympathetic, he lives in the Solar Palace. He is unmarried but a mighty lover; uninhibited, but a charming host and devoted friend; democratic, but the feudal overlord of a bankrupt Family of Planets that suffers misgovernment, oppression, poverty, and confusion with a cheerful joy that sings nothing but Hosannas to the glory of Oddy Gaul.

In a last moment of clarity, Jesse Migg communicated his desolate summation of the situation to his friends in the Faculty Club. This was shortly before they made the trip to join Oddy in the palace as his confidential and valued advisers.

"We were fools," Migg said bitterly. "We should have killed him. He isn't an angel. He's a monster. Civilization and culture . . . philosophy and ethics . . . those were only masks Oddy put on; masks that covered the primitive impulses of his subconscious mind."

"You mean Oddy was not sincere?" Johansen asked heavily. "He wanted this wreckage . . . this ruin?"

"Certainly he was sincere . . . consciously. He still is. He thinks he desires nothing but the most good for the most men. He's honest, kind and generous . . . but only consciously."

"Ah! The Id!" said Hrrdnikkisch with an explosion of breath as though he had been punched in the stomach.

"You understand, Signoid? I see you do. Gentlemen, we were imbeciles. We made the mistake of assuming that Oddy would have conscious control of his power. He does not. The control was and still is below the thinking, reasoning level. The control lies in Oddy's Id . . . in that deep unconscious reservoir of primordial selfishness that lies within every man."

"Then he wanted the war," Bellanby said.

"His Id wanted the war, Bellanby. It was the quickest route to what his Id desires . . . to be Lord of the Universe and loved by the Universe . . . and his Id controls the Power. All of us have that selfish, egocentric Id within us, perpetually searching for satisfaction, timeless, immortal, knowing no logic, no values, no good and evil, no morality; and that is what controls the power in Oddy. He will always win, not what he's been educated to desire but what his Id desires. It's the inescapable conflict that may be the doom of our system."

"But we'll be there to advise him . . . counsel him . . . guide him," Bellanby protested. "He's asked us to come."

"And he'll listen to our advice like the good child that he is," Migg answered, "agreeing with us, trying to make a heaven for everybody while his Id will be making a hell for everybody. Oddy isn't unique. We all suffer from the same conflict . . . but Oddy has the power."

"What can we do?" Johansen groaned. "What can we do?"

"I don't know." Migg bit his lip, then bobbed his head to Papa Johansen in what amounted to apology for him. "Johansen," he said, "you were right. There must be a God, if only because there must be an opposite to Oddy Gaul, who was most assuredly invented by the Devil."

But that was Jesse Migg's last sane statement. Now, of course, he adores Gaul the Glorious, Gaul the Gauleiter, Gaul the God Eternal who has achieved the savage, selfish satisfaction for which all of us unconsciously yearn from birth, but which only Oddy Gaul has won.

THE MAN WITH ENGLISH

Horace L. Gold

Most of the strange gifts with which the characters in this book are blessed or afflicted came to them as accidents of birth, genetic twists of fate. But not all gifts are inherited ones; some are simply thrust upon one in the course of life. As was the case with the hapless Edgar Stone, who went into the hospital with one problem and came out with . . . well, another.

Horace L. Gold is a veteran writer and editor who lives in southern California. Among his best-known stories are "Trouble With Water," "A Matter of Form," and "The Old Die Rich." As the creative and dynamic editor of Galaxy Magazine, *which he founded in 1950, he was for many years a dominant figure in the shaping of contemporary science fiction.*

Lying in the hospital, Edgar Stone added up his misfortunes as another might count blessings. There were enough to infuriate the most temperate man, which Stone notoriously was not. He smashed his fist down, accidentally hitting the metal side of the bed, and was astonished by the pleasant feeling. It enraged him even more. The really maddening thing was how simply he had goaded himself into the hospital.

He'd locked up his drygoods store and driven home for lunch. Nothing unusual about that; he did it every day. With his miserable digestion, he couldn't stand the restaurant food in town. He pulled into the driveway, rode over a collection of metal shapes his son Arnold had left lying around, and punctured a tire.

"Rita!" he yelled. "This is going too damned far! Where is that brat?"

"In here," she called truculently from the kitchen.

He kicked open the screen door. His foot went through the mesh.

"A ripped tire and a torn screen!" he shouted at Arnold, who was sprawled in angular adolescence over a blueprint on the kitchen table. "You'll pay for them, by God! They're coming out of your allowance!"

"I'm sorry, Pop," the boy said.

"Sorry, my left foot," Mrs. Stone shrieked. She whirled on her husband. "You could have watched where you were going. He promised to clean up his things from the driveway right after lunch. And it's about time you stopped kicking open the door every time you're mad."

"Mad? Who wouldn't be mad? Me hoping he'd get out of school and come into the store, and he wants to be an engineer. An engineer—and he can't even make change when he—hah!—helps me out in the store!"

"He'll be whatever he wants to be," she screamed in the conversational tone of the Stone household.

"Please," said Arnold. "I can't concentrate on this plan."

Edgar Stone was never one to restrain an angry impulse. He tore up the blueprint and flung the pieces down on the table.

"Aw, Pop!" Arnold protested.

"Don't say 'Aw, Pop' to me. You're not going to waste a summer vacation on junk like this. You'll eat your lunch and come down to the store. And you'll do it every day for the rest of the summer!"

"Oh, he will, will he?" demanded Mrs. Stone. "He'll catch up on his studies. And as for you, you can go back and eat in a restaurant."

"You know I can't stand that slop!"

"You'll eat it because you're not having lunch here any more. I've got enough to do without making three meals a day."

"But I can't drive back with that tire—"

He did, though not with the tire—he took a cab. It cost a dollar plus tip, lunch was a dollar and a half plus tip, bicarb at Rite Drug Store a few doors away and in a great hurry came to another fifteen cents—only it didn't work.

And then Miss Ellis came in for some material. Miss Ellis could round out any miserable day. She was fifty, tall, skinny and had thin, disapproving lips. She had a sliver of cloth clipped very meagerly off a hem that she intended to use as a sample.

"The arms of the slipcover on my reading chair wore through," she informed him. "I bought the material here, if you remember."

Stone didn't have to look at the fragmentary swatch. "That was about seven years ago—"

"Six and a half," she corrected. "I paid enough for it. You'd expect anything that expensive to last."

"The style was discontinued. I have something here that—"

"I do not want to make an entire slipcover, Mr. Stone. All I want is enough to make new panels for the arms. Two yards should do very nicely."

Stone smothered a bilious hiccup. "Two yards, Miss Ellis?"

"At the most."

"I sold the last of that material years ago." He pulled a bolt off a shelf and partly unrolled it for her. "Why not use a different pattern as a kind of contrast?"

"I want this same pattern," she said, her thin lips getting even thinner and more obstinate.

"Then I'll have to order it and hope one of my wholesalers still has some of it in stock."

"Not without looking for it first right here, you won't order it for me. You can't know *all* these materials you have on these shelves."

Stone felt all the familiar symptoms of fury—the sudden pulsing of the temples, the lurch and bump of his heart as adrenalin came surging in like the tide at the Firth of Forth, the quivering of his hands, the angry shout pulsing at his vocal cords from below.

"I'll take a look, Miss Ellis," he said.

She was president of the Ladies' Cultural Society and dominated it so thoroughly that the members would go clear to the next town for their dry goods, rather than deal with him, if he offended this sour stick of stubbornness.

If Stone's life insurance salesman had been there, he would have tried to keep Stone from climbing the ladder that ran around the three walls of the store. He probably wouldn't have been in time. Stone stamped up the ladder to reach the highest shelves, where there were scraps of bolts. One of them might have been the remnant of the material Miss Ellis had bought six and a half years ago. But Stone never found out.

He snatched one, glaring down meanwhile at the top of Miss Ellis's head, and the ladder skidded out from under him. He felt his skull collide with the counter. He didn't feel it hit the floor.

"God damn it!" Stone yelled. "You could at least turn on the lights."

"There, there, Edgar. Everything's fine, just fine."

It was his wife's voice and the tone was so uncommonly soft and soothing that it scared him into a panic.

"What's wrong with me?" he asked piteously. "Am I blind?"

"How many fingers am I holding up?" a man wanted to know.

Stone was peering into the blackness. All he could see before his eyes was a vague blot against a darker blot.

"None," he bleated. "Who are you?"

"Dr. Rankin. That was a nasty fall you had, Mr. Stone—concussion, of course, and a splinter of bone driven into the brain. I had to operate to remove it."

"Then you cut out a nerve!" Stone said. "You did something to my eyes!"

The doctor's voice sounded puzzled. "There doesn't seem to be anything wrong with them. I'll take a look, though, and see."

"You'll be all right, dear," Mrs. Stone said reassuringly, but she didn't sound as if she believed it.

"Sure you will, Pop," said Arnold.

"Is that young stinker here?" Stone demanded. "He's the cause of all this!"

"Temper, temper," the doctor said. "Accidents happen."

Stone heard him lower the venetian blinds. As if they had been a switch, light sprang up and everything in the hospital room became brightly visible.

"Well!" said Stone. "That's more like it. It's night and you're trying to save electricity, hey?"

"It's broad daylight, Edgar dear," his wife protested. "All Dr. Rankin did was lower the blinds and—"

"Please," the doctor said. "If you don't mind, I'd rather take care of any explanations that have to be made."

He came at Stone with an ophthalmoscope. When he flashed it into Stone's eyes, everything went black and Stone let him know it vociferously.

"Black?" Dr. Rankin repeated blankly. "Are you positive? Not a sudden glare?"

"Black," insisted Stone. "And what's the idea of putting me in a bed filled with bread crumbs?"

"It was freshly made—"

"Crumbs. You heard me. And the pillow has rocks in it."

"What else is bothering you?" asked the doctor worriedly.

"It's freezing in here." Stone felt the terror rise in him again. "It was summer when I fell off the ladder. Don't tell me I've been unconscious clear through till winter!"

"No, Pop," said Arnold. "That was yesterday—"

"I'll take care of this," Dr. Rankin said firmly. "I'm afraid you and your son will have to leave, Mrs. Stone. I have to do a few tests on your husband."

"Will he be all right?" she appealed.

"Of course, of course," he said inattentively, peering with a frown at the shivering patient. "Shock, you know," he added vaguely.

"Gosh, Pop," said Arnold. "I'm sorry this happened. I got the driveway all cleaned up."

"And we'll take care of the store till you're better," Mrs. Stone promised.

"Don't you dare!" yelled Stone. "You'll put me out of business!"

The doctor hastily shut the door on them and came back to the bed. Stone was clutching the light summer blanket around himself. He felt colder than he'd ever been in his life.

"Can't you get me more blankets?" he begged. "You don't want me to die of pneumonia, do you?"

Dr. Rankin opened the blinds and asked, "What's this like?"

"Night," chattered Stone. "A new idea to save electricity—hooking up the blinds to the light switch?"

The doctor closed the blinds and sat down beside the bed. He was sweating as he reached for the signal button and pressed it. A nurse came in, blinking in their direction.

"Why don't you turn on the light?" she asked.

"Huh?" said Stone. "They are."

"Nurse, I'm Dr. Rankin. Get me a piece of sandpaper, some cotton swabs, an ice cube, and Mr. Stone's lunch."

"Is there anything he shouldn't eat?"

"That's what I want to find out. Hurry, please."

"And some blankets," Stone put in, shaking with the chill.

"Blankets, Doctor?" she asked, startled.

"Half a dozen will do," he said. "I think."

It took her ten minutes to return with all the items. Stone wanted them to keep adding blankets until all seven were on him. He still felt cold.

"Maybe some hot coffee?" he suggested.

The doctor nodded and the nurse poured a cup, added the spoon and a half of sugar he requested, and he took a mouthful. He sprayed it out violently.

"Ice cold!" he yelped. "And who put salt in it?"

"Salt?" She fumbled around on the tray. "It's so dark here—"

"I'll attend to it," Dr. Rankin said hurriedly. "Thank you."

She walked cautiously to the door and went out.

"Try this," said the doctor, after filling another cup.

"Well, that's better!" Stone exclaimed. "Damned practical joker. They shouldn't be allowed to work in hospitals."

"And now, if you don't mind," said the doctor, "I'd like to try several tests."

Stone was still angry at the trick played on him, but he cooperated willingly.

Dr. Rankin finally sagged back in the chair. The sweat ran

down his face and into his collar, and his expression was so dazed that Stone was alarmed.

"What's wrong, Doctor? Am I going to–going to–"

"No, no. It's not that. No danger. At least, I don't believe there is. But I can't even be sure of that any more."

"You can't be sure if I'll live or die?"

"Look." Dr. Rankin grimly pulled the chair closer. "It's broad daylight and yet you can't see until I darken the room. The coffee was hot and sweet, but it was cold and salty to you, so I added an ice cube and a spoonful of salt and it tasted fine, you said. This is one of the hottest days on record and you're freezing. You told me the sandpaper felt smooth and satiny, then yelled that somebody had put pins in the cotton swabs, when there weren't any, of course. I've tried you out with different colors around the room and you saw violet when you should have seen yellow, green for red, orange for blue, and so on. Now do you understand?"

"No," said Stone frightenedly. "What's wrong?"

"All I can do is guess. I had to remove that sliver of bone from your brain. It apparently shorted your sensory nerves."

"And what happened?"

"Every one of your senses has been reversed. You feel cold for heat, heat for cold, smooth for rough, rough for smooth, sour for sweet, sweet for sour, and so forth. And you see colors backward."

Stone sat up. "Murderer! Thief! You've ruined me!"

The doctor sprang for a hypodermic and sedative. Just in time, he changed his mind and took a bottle of stimulant instead. It worked fine, though injecting it into his screaming, thrashing patient took more strength than he'd known he owned. Stone fell asleep immediately.

There were nine blankets on Stone and he had a bag of cement for a pillow when he had his lawyer, Manny Lubin, in to hear the charges he wanted brought against Dr. Rankin. The doctor was there to defend himself. Mrs. Stone was present in spite of her husband's objections– "She always takes everybody's side against me," he explained in a roar.

"I'll be honest with you, Mr. Lubin," the doctor said, after Stone had finished on a note of shrill frustration. "I've hunted for cases like this in medical history and this is the first one ever to be reported. Except," he amended quickly, "that I haven't reported it yet. I'm hoping it reverses itself. That sometimes happens, you know."

"And what am I supposed to do in the meantime?" raged Stone. "I'll have to go out wearing an overcoat in the summer and shorts in the winter—people will think I'm a maniac. And they'll be *sure* of it because I'll have to keep the store closed during the day and open at night—I can't see except in the dark. And matching materials! I can't stand the feel of smooth cloth and I see colors backward!" He glared at the doctor before turning back to Lubin. "How would *you* like to have to put sugar on your food and salt in your coffee?"

"But we'll work it out, Edgar dear," his wife soothed. "Arnold and I can take care of the store. You always wanted him to come into the business, so that ought to please you—"

"As long as I'm there to watch him!"

"And Dr. Rankin said maybe things will straighten out."

"What about that, Doctor?" asked Lubin. "What are the chances?"

Dr. Rankin looked uncomfortable. "I don't know. This has never happened before. All we can do is hope."

"Hope, nothing!" Stone stormed. "I want to sue him. He had no right to go meddling around and turn me upside down. Any jury would give me a quarter of a million!"

"I'm no millionaire, Mr. Stone," said the doctor.

"But the hospital has money. We'll sue him and the trustees."

There was a pause while the attorney thought. "I'm afraid we wouldn't have a case, Mr. Stone." He went on more rapidly as Stone sat up, shivering. "Any surgeon would have had to operate. Am I right, Dr. Rankin?"

The doctor explained what would have happened if he had not removed the pressure on the brain, resulting from the concussion, and the danger that the bone splinter, if not extracted, might have gone on traveling and caused possible paralysis or death.

"That would be better than this," said Stone.

"But medical ethics couldn't allow him to let you die," Lubin objected. "He was doing his duty. That's point one."

"Mr. Lubin is absolutely right, Edgar," said Mrs. Stone.

"There, you see?" screamed her husband. "Everybody's right but me! Will you get her out of here before I have a stroke?"

"Her interests are also involved," Lubin pointed out. "Point two is that the emergency came first; the aftereffects couldn't be known or considered."

Dr. Rankin brightened. "Any operation involves risk, even the excising of a corn. I had to take those risks."

"*You* had to take them?" Stone scoffed. "All right, what are you leading up to, Lubin?"

"We'd lose," said the attorney.

Stone subsided, but only for a moment. "So we'll lose. But if we sue, the publicity would ruin him. I want to sue!"

"For what, Edgar dear?" his wife persisted. "We'll have a hard enough time managing. Why throw good money after bad?"

"Why didn't I marry a woman who'd take my side, even when I'm wrong?" moaned Stone. "Revenge, that's what. And he won't be able to practice, so he'll have time to find out if there's a cure . . . and at no charge, either! I won't pay him another cent!"

The doctor stood up eagerly. "But I'm willing to see what can be done right now. And it wouldn't cost you anything, naturally."

"What do you mean?" Stone challenged suspiciously.

"If I were to perform another operation, I'll be able to see which nerves were involved. There's no need to go into the technical side right now, but it is possible to connect nerves. Of course, there are a good many, which complicates matters, especially since the splinter went through several layers—"

Lubin pointed a lawyer's impaling finger at him. "Are you offering to attempt to correct the injury—gratis?"

"Certainly. I mean to say, I'll do my absolute best. But keep in mind, please, that there is no medical precedent."

The attorney, however, was already questioning Stone and his wife. "In view of the fact that we have no legal grounds whatever for suit, does this offer of settlement satisfy your claim against him?"

"Oh, yes!" Mrs. Stone cried.

Her husband hesitated for a while, clearly tempted to take the opposite position out of habit. "I guess so," he reluctantly agreed.

"Well, then it's in your hands, Doctor," said Lubin.

Dr. Rankin buzzed excitedly for the nurse. "I'll have him prepared for surgery right away."

"It better work this time," warned Stone, clutching a handful of ice cubes to warm his fingers.

Stone came to foggily. He didn't know it, but he had given the anesthetist a bewildering problem, which finally had been solved by using fumes of aromatic spirits of ammonia. The four blurred figures around the bed seemed to be leaning precariously toward him.

"Pop!" said Arnold. "Look, he's coming out of it! Pop!"

"Speak to me, Edgar dear," Mrs. Stone beseeched.

Lubin said, "See how he is, Doctor."

"He's fine," the doctor insisted heartily, his usual bedside manner evidently having returned. "He must be—the blinds are open and he's not complaining that it's dark or that he's cold." He leaned over the bed. "How are we feeling, Mr. Stone?"

It took a minute or two for Stone to move his swollen tongue enough to answer. He wrinkled his nose in disgust.

"What smells purple?" he demanded.

TO BE CONTINUED

Robert Silverberg

Imagine what it's like to be almost immortal—to have a lifespan measured in centuries instead of years. To live on and on while friends and relatives grow old, while empires fall, while whole civilizations crumble. Such immortality can be a precious gift—but it must be concealed from the short-lived ones, who would fear and resent the existence of immortals. But what's the best method of disguise?

Gaius Titus Menenius sat thoughtfully in his oddly decorated apartment on Park Avenue, staring at the envelope that had just arrived. He contemplated it for a moment, noting with amusement that he was actually somewhat perturbed over the possible nature of its contents.

After a moment he elbowed up from the red contour chair and crossed the room in three bounds. Still holding the envelope, he eased himself down on the long green couch near the wall, and extending himself full-length, slit the envelope open with a neat flick of his fingernail. The medical report was within, as he had expected.

"Dear Mr. Riswell," it read. "I am herewith enclosing a copy of the laboratory report concerning your examination last week. I am pleased to report that our findings are positive—emphatically so. In view of our conversation, I am sure this finding will be extremely pleasing to you, and, of course, to your wife. Sincerely, F. D. Rowcliff, M.D."

Menenius read the letter through once again, examined the enclosed report, and allowed his face to open in a wide grin. It was almost an anticlimax, after all these centuries. He couldn't bring himself to become very excited over it—not any more.

He stood up and stretched happily. "Well, Mr. Riswell," he said to himself, "I think this calls for a drink. In fact, a night on the town."

He chose a smart dinner jacket from his wardrobe and moved toward the door. It swung open at his approach. He went out into the corridor and disappeared into the elevator, whistling gaily, his mind full of new plans and new thoughts.

It was a fine feeling. After two thousand years of waiting, he had finally achieved his maturity. He could have a child. At last!

"Good afternoon, Mr. Schuyler," said the barman. "Will it be the usual, sir?"

"Martini, of course," said W. M. Schuyler IV, seating himself casually on the padded stool in front of the bar.

Behind the projected personality of W. M. Schuyler IV, Gaius Titus smiled, mentally. W. M. Schuyler *always* drank martinis. And they had pretty well better be dry—very dry.

The baroque strains of a Vivaldi violin concerto sang softly in the background. Schuyler watched the TV accompaniment—a dancing swirl of colors that moved with the music.

"Good afternoon, Miss Vanderpool," he heard the barman say. "An old-fashioned?"

Schuyler took another sip of his martini and looked up. The girl had appeared suddenly and had taken the seat next to him, looking her usual cool self.

"Sharon!" he said, putting just the right amount of exclamation point after it.

She turned to look at him and smiled, disclosing a brilliantly white array of perfect teeth. "Bill! I didn't notice you! How long have you been here?"

"Just arrived," Schuyler told her. "Just about a minute ago."

The barman put her drink down in front of her. She took a long sip without removing her eyes from him. Schuyler met her glance, and behind his eyes Gaius Titus was coldly appraising her in a new light.

He had met her in Kavanaugh's a month before, and he had readily enough added her to the string. Why not? She was young, pretty, intelligent, and made a pleasant companion. There had been others like her—a thousand others, two thousand, five thousand. One gets to meet quite a few in two millennia.

Only now Gaius Titus was finally mature, and had different needs. The string of girls to which Sharon belonged was going to be cut.

He wanted a wife.

"How's the lackey of Wall Street?" Sharon asked. "Still coining money faster than you know how to spend it?"

"I'll leave that for you to decide," he said. He signaled for two more drinks. "Care to take in a concert tonight? The Bach Group's giving a benefit this evening, you know, and I'm told there still are a few hundred-dollar seats left—"

There, Gaius Titus thought. The bait has been cast. She ought to respond.

She whistled, a long, low, sophisticated whistle. "I'd venture that business is fairly good, then," she said. Her eyes fell. "But I don't want to let you go to all that expense on my account, Bill."

"It's nothing," Schuyler insisted, while Gaius Titus continued to weigh her in the balance. "They're doing the Fourth Brandenburg, and Renoli's playing the Goldberg Variations. How about?"

She met his gaze evenly. "Sorry, Bill. I have something else on for the evening." Her tone left no doubt in Schuyler's mind that there was little point pressing the discussion any further. Gaius Titus felt a sharp pang of disappointment.

Schuyler lifted his hand, palm forward. "Say no more! I should have known you'd be booked up for tonight already." He paused. "What about tomorrow?" he asked, after a moment. "There's a reading of Webster's 'Duchess of Malfi' down at the Dramatist's League. It's been one of my favorite plays for a long time."

Silently smiling, he waited for her reply. The Webster was, indeed, a long-time favorite. Gaius Titus recalled having attended one of its first performances, during his short employ in the court of James I. During the next three and a half centuries, he had formed a sentimental attachment for the creaky old melodrama.

"Not tomorrow either," Sharon said. "Some other night, Bill."

"All right," he said. "Some other night."

He reached out a hand and put it over hers, and they fell silent, listening to the Vivaldi in the background. He contemplated her high, sharp cheekbones in the purple half-light, wondering if she could be the one to bear the child he had waited for so long.

She had parried all his thrusts in a fashion that surprised him. She was not at all impressed by his display of wealth and culture. Titus reflected sadly that, perhaps, his Schuyler facet had been inadequate for her.

No, he thought, rejecting the idea. The haunting slow movement of the Vivaldi faded to its end and a lively allegro took its place. No; he had had too much experience in calculating personality-facets to fit the individual to have erred. He was certain that W. M. Schuyler IV was capable of handling Sharon.

For the first few hundred years of his unexpectedly long life, Gaius Titus had been forced to adopt the practice of turning on and off different personalities as a matter of mere survival. Things had been easy for a while after the fall of Rome, but with the coming of the Middle Ages he had needed all his skill to keep from running afoul of the superstitious. He had carefully built up a series of masks, of false fronts, as a survival mechanism.

How many times had he heard someone tell him, in jest, "You ought to be on the stage"? It struck home. He *was* on the stage. He was a man of many roles. Somewhere, beneath it all, was the unalterable personality of Gaius Titus Menenius, *cives Romanus,* casting the shadows that were his many masks. But Gaius Titus was far below the surface—the surface which, at the moment, was W. M. Schuyler IV; which had been Preston Riswell the week before, when he had visited the doctor for that fateful examination; which could be Leslie MacGregor or Sam Spielman or Phil Carlson tomorrow, depending on where Gaius Titus was, in what circumstances, and talking to whom. There was only one person he did not dare to be, and that was himself.

He wasn't immortal; he knew that. But he was *relatively* immortal. His life-span was tremendously decelerated, and it had taken him two thousand years to become, physically, a fertile adult. His span was roughly a hundred times that of a normal man's. And, according to what he had learned in the last century, his longevity should be transmissible genetically. All he needed now was someone to transmit it to.

Was it dominant? That he didn't know. That was the gamble he'd be making. He wondered what it would be like to watch his children and his children's children shrivel with age. Not pleasant, he thought.

The conversation with Sharon lagged; it was obvious that something was wrong with his Schuyler facet, at least so far as she was concerned, though he was unable to see where the trouble lay. After a few more minutes of disjointed chatter, she excused herself and left the bar. He watched her go. She had eluded him neatly. Where to next?

He thought he knew.

The East End Bar was far downtown and not very reputable. Gaius Titus pushed through the revolving door and headed for the counter.

"Hi, Sam. Howsa boy?" the bartender said.

"Let's have a beer, Jerry." The bartender shoved a beer out toward the short, swarthy man in the leather jacket.

"Things all right?"

"Can't complain, Jerry. How's business?" Sam Spielman asked, as he lifted the beer to his mouth.

"It's lousy."

"It figures," Sam said. "Why don't you put in automatics? They're getting all the business now."

"Sure, Sam, sure. And where do I get the dough? That's

twenty." He took the coins Sam dropped on the bar and grinned. "At least you can afford beer."

"You know me, Jerry," Sam said. "My credit's good."

Jerry nodded. "Good enough." He punched the coins into the register. "Ginger was looking for you, by the way. What you got against the gal?"

"Against her? Nothin'. What do y'mean?" Sam pushed out his beer shell for a refill.

"She's got a hook out for you—you know that, don't you?" Jerry was grinning.

Gaius Titus thought: *She's not very bright, but she might very well serve my purpose. She has other characteristics worth transmitting.*

"Hi, Sammy."

He turned to look at her. "Hi, Ginger," he said. "How's the gal?"

"Not bad, honey." But she didn't look it. She looked as though she'd been dragged through the mill. Her blond hair was disarranged, her blouse was wrinkled, and, as usual, her teeth were discolored by the lipstick that had rubbed off on them.

"I love you, Sammy," she said softly.

"I love you, too," Sam said. He meant it.

Gaius Titus thought sourly: *But how many of her characteristics would I not want to transmit? Still, she'll do, I guess. She's a solid girl.*

"Sam," she said, interrupting the flow of his thoughts, "why don't you come around more often? I miss you."

"Look, Ginger baby," Sam said. "Remember, I've got a long haul to pull. If I marry you, you gotta understand that I don't get home often. I gotta drive a truck. You might not see me more than once or twice a week."

Titus rubbed his forehead. He wasn't quite sure, after all, that the girl was worthwhile. She had spunk, all right, but was she worthy of fostering a race of immortals?

He didn't get a chance to find out. "Married?" The blonde's voice sounded incredulous. "Who the devil wants to get married?

You've got me on the wrong track, Sam. I don't want to get myself tied down."

"Sure, honey, sure," he said. "But I thought—"

Ginger stood up. "You think anything you please, Sam. Anything you please. But not marriage."

She stared at him hard for a moment, and walked off. Sam looked after her morosely.

Gaius Titus grinned behind the Sam Spielman mask. She wasn't the girl either. Two thousand years of life had taught him that women were unpredictable, and he wasn't altogether surprised at her reaction to his proposal.

But he was disturbed over this second failure of the evening nevertheless. Was his judgment that far off? Perhaps, he thought, he was losing the vital ability of personality-projection. He didn't like that idea.

For hours, Gaius Titus walked the streets of New York.

New York. Sure it was new. So was Old York, in England. Menenius had seen both of them grow from tiny villages to towns to cities to metropoli.

Metropoli. That was Greek. It had taken him twelve years to learn Greek. He hadn't rushed it.

Twelve years. And he still wasn't an adult. He could remember when the Emperor had seen the sign in the sky: *In hoc signo vinces.* And, at the age of four hundred and sixty-two, he'd still been too young to enter the service of the Empire.

Gaius Titus Menenius, Citizen of Rome. When he had been a child, he had thought Rome would last forever. But it hadn't; Rome had fallen. Egypt, which he had long thought of as an empire which would last forever, had gone even more quickly. It had died and putrefied and sloughed off into the Great River which carries all life off into death.

Over the years and the centuries, races and peoples and nations had come and gone. And their passing had had no effect at all on Gaius Titus.

He was walking north. He turned left on Market Street, away

from the Manhattan Bridge. Suddenly, he was tired of walking. He hailed a passing taxi.

He gave the cabby his address on Park Avenue and leaned back against the cushions to relax.

The first few centuries had been hard. He hadn't grown up, in the first place. By the time he was twenty, he had attained his full height—five feet nine. But he still looked like a seventeen-year-old.

And he had still looked that way nineteen hundred years later. It had been a long, hard drive to make enough money to live on during that time. Kids don't get well-paying jobs.

Actually, he'd lived a miserable hand-to-mouth existence for centuries. But the gradual collapse of the Christian ban on usury had opened the way for him to make some real money. Money makes more money, in a capitalistic system, if you have patience. Titus had time on his side.

It wasn't until the free-enterprise system had evolved that he started to get anywhere. But a deposit of several hundred pounds in the proper firm back in 1735 had netted a little extra money. The British East India Company had brought his financial standing up a great deal, and judicious investments ever since left him comfortably fixed. He derived considerable amusement from the extraordinary effects compound interest exerted on a bank account a century old.

"Here you are, buddy," said the cab driver.

Gaius Titus climbed out and gave the driver a five note without asking for change.

Zeus, he thought. *I might as well make a night of it.*

He hadn't been really drunk since the stock market collapse back in 1929.

Leslie MacGregor pushed open the door of the San Marino Bar in Greenwich Village and walked to the customary table in the back corner. Three people were already there, and the conversation was going well. Leslie waved a hand and the two men waved back. The girl grinned and beckoned.

"Come on over, Les," she yelled across the noisy room. "Mack has just sold a story!" Her deep voice was clear and firm.

Mack, the heavy-set man next to the wall, grinned self-consciously and picked up his beer.

Leslie strolled quietly over to the booth and sat down beside Corwyn, the odd man of the trio.

"Sold a story?" Leslie repeated archly.

Mack nodded. "*Chimerical Review*," he said. "A little thing I called 'Pluck Up the Torch.' Not much, but it's a sale, you know."

"If one wants to prostitute one's art," said Corwyn.

Leslie frowned at him. "Don't be snide. After all, Mack has to pay his rent." Then he turned toward the girl. "Lorraine, could I talk to you a moment?"

She brushed the blond hair back from the shoulders of her black turtleneck sweater and widened the grin on her face.

"Sure, Les," she said in her oddly deep, almost masculine voice. "What's all the big secret?"

No secret, thought Gaius Titus. What I want is simple enough.

For a long time, he had thought that near-immortality carried with it the curse of sterility. Now he knew it was simply a matter of time—of growing up.

As he stood up to walk to the bar with Lorraine, he caught a glimpse of himself in the dusty mirror behind the bar. He didn't look much over twenty-five. But things had been changing in the past fifty years. He had never had a heavy beard before; he had not developed his husky baritone voice until a year before the outbreak of the First World War.

It had been difficult, at first, to hide his immortality. Changing names, changing residences, changing, changing, changing. Until he had found that he didn't have to change—not deep inside.

People don't recognize faces. Faces are essentially all alike. Two eyes, two ears, a nose, a mouth. What more is there to a face? Only the personality behind it.

A personality is something that is projected—something put on for display for others to see. And Gaius Titus Menenius had found that two thousand years of experience had given him enough internal psychological reality to be able to project any personality he wanted to. All he needed was a change of dress and a change of personality to be a different person. His face changed subtly to fit the person who was wearing it; no one had ever caught on.

Lorraine sat down on the bar stool. "Beer," she said to the bartender. "What's the matter, Les? What's eating you?"

He studied her firm, strong features, her deep, mocking eyes. "Lorraine," he said softly, "will you marry me?"

She blinked. "Marry you? You? Marry?" She grinned again. "Who'd ever think it? A bourgeois conformist, like all the rest." Then she shook her head. "No, Les. Even if you're kidding, you ought to know better than that. What's the gag?"

"No gag," said Leslie, and Gaius Titus fought his surprise and shock at his third failure. "I see your point," Leslie said. "Forget it. Give my best to everyone." He got up without his beer and walked out the door.

Leslie stepped out into the street and started heading for the subway. Then Gaius Titus, withdrawing the mask, checked himself and hailed a cab.

He got into the cab and gave the driver his home address. He didn't see any reason for further pursuing his adventures that evening.

He was mystified. How could *three* personality-facets fail so completely? He had been handling these three girls well ever since he had met them, but tonight, going from one to the next, as soon as he made any serious ventures toward any of them, the whole thing folded. Why?

"It's a lousy world," he told the driver, assuming for the moment the mask of Phil Carlson, cynical newsman. "Damn lousy." His voice was a biting rasp.

"What's wrong, buddy?"

"Had a fight with all three of my girls. It's a lousy world."

"I'll buy that," the driver said. The cab swung up into Park. "But look at it this way, pal: who needs them?"

For a moment the mask blurred and fell aside, and it was Gaius Titus, not Phil Carlson, who said, "That's exactly right! Who needs them?" He gave the driver a bill and got out of the cab.

Who needs them? It was a good question. There were plenty of girls. Why should he saddle himself with Sharon, or Ginger, or Lorraine? They all had their good qualities—Sharon's social grace, Ginger's vigor and drive, Lorraine's rugged intellectualism. They were all three good-looking girls, tall, attractive, well put together. But yet each one, he realized, lacked something that the others had. None of them was really *worthy* by herself, he thought, apologizing to himself for what another man might call conceit, or sour grapes.

None of them would really do. But if somehow, some way, he could manage to combine those three leggy girls, those three personalities into one body, *there* would be a girl—

He gasped.

He whirled and caught sight of the cab he had just vacated.

"Hey, cabby!" Titus called. "Come back here! Take me back to the San Marino!"

She wasn't there. As Leslie burst in, he caught sight of Corwyn, sitting alone and grinning twistedly over a beer.

"Where'd they go? Where's Lorraine?"

The little man lifted his shoulders and eyebrows in an elaborate shrug. "They left about a minute ago. No, it was closer to ten, wasn't it? They went in separate directions. They left me here."

"Thanks," Leslie said.

Scratch Number One, Titus thought. He ran to the phone booth in the back, dialed Information, and demanded the number of the East End Bar. After some fumbling, the operator found it.

He dialed. The bartender's tired face appeared in the screen.

"Hello, Sam," the barkeep said. "What's doing?"

"Do me a favor, Jerry," Sam said. "Look around your place for Ginger."

"She ain't here, Sam," the bartender said. "Haven't seen her since you two blew out of here a while back." Jerry's eyes narrowed. "I ain't never seen you dressed up like that before, Sam, you know?"

Gaius Titus crouched down suddenly to get out of range of the screen. "I'm celebrating tonight, Jerry," he said, and broke the connection.

Ginger wasn't to be found either, eh? That left only Sharon. He couldn't call Kavanaugh's—they wouldn't give a caller any information about their patrons. Grabbing another taxi, he shot across town to Kavanaugh's.

Sharon wasn't there when Schuyler entered. She hadn't been in since the afternoon, a waiter informed him, after receiving a small gratuity. Schuyler had a drink and left. Gaius Titus returned to his apartment, tingling with an excitement he hadn't known for centuries.

He returned to Kavanaugh's the next night, and the next. Still no sign of her.

The following evening, though, when he entered the bar, she was sitting there, nursing an old-fashioned. He slid onto the seat next to her. She looked up in surprise.

"Bill! Good to see you again."

"The same here," Gaius Titus said. "It's good to see you again—Ginger. Or is it Lorraine?"

She paled and put her hand to her mouth. Then, covering, she said, "What do you mean, Bill? Have you had too many drinks tonight?"

"Possibly," Titus said. "I stopped off in the San Marino before I came up. You weren't there, Lorraine. That deep voice is quite a trick, I have to admit. I had a drink with Mack and Corwyn. Then I went over to the East End, Ginger. You weren't there, either. So," he said, "there was only one place left to find you, Sharon."

She stared at him for a long moment. Finally she said, simply, "Who are you?"

"Leslie MacGregor," Titus said. "Also Sam Spielman. And W. M. Schuyler. Plus two or three other people. The name is Gaius Titus Menenius, at your service."

"I still don't understand—"

"Yes, you do," Titus said. "You are clever—but not clever enough. Your little game had me going for almost a month, you know? And it's not easy to fool a man my age."

"When did you find out?" the girl asked weakly.

"Monday night, when I saw all three of you within a couple of hours."

"You're—"

"Yes. I'm like you," he said. "But I'll give you credit: I didn't see through it until I was on my way home. You were using my own camouflage technique against me, and I didn't spot it for what it was. What's your real name?"

"Mary Bradford," she said. "I was English, originally. Of fine Plantagenet stock. I'm really a Puritan at heart, you see." She was grinning slyly.

"Oh? *Mayflower* descendant?" Titus asked teasingly.

"No," Mary replied. "Not a descendant. A passenger. And I'll tell you—I was awfully happy to get out of England and over here to Plymouth Colony."

He toyed with her empty glass. "You didn't like England? Probably my fault. I was a minor functionary in King James's court in the early seventeenth century."

They giggled together over it. Titus stared at her, his pulse pounding harder and harder. She stared back. Her eyes were smiling.

"I didn't think there was another one," she said after a while. "It was so strange, never growing old. I was afraid they'd burn me as a witch. I had to keep changing, moving all the time. It wasn't a pleasant life. It's better lately—I enjoy these little poses. But I'm glad you caught on to me," she said. She reached out and took his hand. "I guess I would never have been smart enough to connect you and Leslie and Sam, the way you did Sharon and Ginger and Lorraine. You play the game too well for me."

"In two thousand years," Titus said, not caring if the waiter overheard him, "I never found another one like me. Believe me, Mary, I looked. I looked hard, and I've had plenty of time to search. And then to find you, hiding behind the faces of three girls I knew!"

He squeezed her hand. The next statement followed logically for him. "Now that we've found each other," he said softly, "we can have a child. A third immortal."

Her face showed radiant enthusiasm. "Wonderful!" she cried. "When can we get married?"

"How about tomor—" he started to say. Then a thought struck him.

"Mary?"

"What . . . Titus?"

"How old did you say you were? When were you born?" he asked.

She thought for a moment. "In 1597," she said. "I'm nearly four hundred."

He nodded, dumb with growing frustration. Only four hundred? That meant—that meant she was now the equivalent of a three-year-old child!

"When can we get married?" she repeated.

"There's no hurry," Titus said dully, letting her hand drop. "We have eleven hundred years."

HUMPTY DUMPTY HAD A GREAT FALL

Frank Belknap Long

Frank Belknap Long is one of science fiction's grand old masters—famous for his dark, somber fantasies and vivid tales of space adventure since the 1930's. His best short stories have been collected in two volumes, The Hounds of Tindalos *and* Rim of the Unknown; *he is also the author of many novels, and has for some time been at work on a biographical study of his friend H. P. Lovecraft, the great weird-tale author.*

"Humpty Dumpty Had a Great Fall," out of print for many years, is considered one of Long's finest works: a mysterious, haunting narrative of other dimensions, of alien beings, of strange images, of an odd young man whose tormented mind is capable of reaching into the universe of nightmares—and of taking others there with him.

Kenneth Wayne was dressing for dinner when he heard the tapping. It was loud, insistent and seemed to be saying: "No use pretending you're not at home, old man! I can hear you moving around in there!"

Wayne groaned. He had no desire to discuss vasomotor psychology with young Graham or polytonal music with the long-haired Dr. Raydel. He was dining out with a charming girl, and he wanted to stay alive, vital, every nerve alert to her beauty.

Wayne was one of those imaginative young men who attract ideas to themselves in the fashion of a baby specialist. Instead of babies, people brought him their budding ideas to admire.

Wayne told himself that he was a fool to be annoyed. The mere sight of his tux draped across a chair should discourage a talkative visitor. With an angry shrug he turned and crossed the room in three long strides. He threw the door wide.

The boy who stood in the doorway was a stranger to him. Boy? Well, it was hard not to think of the youngster as a man, for he was heavily bearded and he carried himself with an air of maturity. But Wayne could see that he wasn't more than eighteen or nineteen years old. His clear blue eyes held the tortured look of the very young, and there was a newness about him which contrasted sharply with Wayne's aspect of world-weariness and cynicism. Wayne was only twenty-seven, but his age rested heavily upon him. His eyes were shadowed and the planes of his face craggy with thought.

"I'm Phillip Orban," the boy said. "I ran away. They were torturing me with their questions."

The Orban boy! Wayne shut his eyes while the universe reeled. Young Orban was carrying an enormous glowing loop of hollow metal. Before Wayne could cry out in protest the trembling lad had stepped into the room and set the loop down on the floor.

"Shut the door," Orban pleaded. "Lock it tight! If they try to get in, tell them I'm not in this room."

Mechanically Wayne locked the door. When he turned, his lips were white.

"Why did you come here?" he demanded. "Do you realize I never saw you before in my life?"

The Orban boy nodded. "I hid in a cellar under an empty house. But I was cold and hungry. I had to come out. A policeman saw me and I had to run for it. I never saw you before, but I like you. You will tell them I'm not here?"

Wayne made a despairing gesture. "All right!" he cried. "Did I say I wouldn't? Just take it easy now. Relax!"

It seemed to Wayne that standing before him was an impossible little gnome with a conical cap on his head, made visible by a dimensional vortex that was about to dissolve in a blaze of light.

That was absurd, of course! The Orban boy wasn't one of those mutant supermen freaks science-fiction writers were always speculating about. He was a quite normal youngster who had been trapped from infancy in the mind-numbing blackness of space.

But what would be the penalty for sheltering a boy with a price on his head, a boy about whom five million words had been written? Young Orban had committed a serious crime. An ugly crime! To get rid of a man by making him disappear was not a whit less ugly than cold-blooded murder!

Wayne stared down at the shining loop of metal, his eyes wide and incredulous. "Is that the machine you built?" he demanded, and was astonished that he could speak at all.

"It's the *door* I built!" Orban said, "I didn't push Dr. Bryce into it. He stumbled and fell."

"But how did you build it?" Wayne prodded. "You never saw a tool."

"There were tools in my father's workshop," Orban said, quickly. "I knew how to build it. Dr. Bryce isn't dead. He's alive in the blue world."

Structurally the machine was an incredibly simple thing. It consisted of a single loop of hollow metal, twisted into a perfect arch like a gigantic croquet wicket. It was easy to see that the loop was hollow, for it was riddled with holes and an eerie radiance was spilling out of it.

"You've got to help me hide it," Orban pleaded. "If I don't get Dr. Bryce out of the blue, bowmen will kill him!"

Wayne turned and gripped the lad's shoulder. "You said you were hungry. Perhaps we can do something about that."

"I am hungry," the lad admitted. "But there's food in the blue world."

Wayne thought that over for a minute; then found himself propelling his guest toward the kitchen.

He left him devouring a glass of milk. No, you didn't devour milk. But the Orban boy was dipping crackers in the milk and eating the crackers. It amounted to the same thing.

Wayne felt that he needed the support of cold print. Actual confirmation of the Orban story in black type. He found the clipping by turning out all the drawers of his desk and then looking under the blotter. It was crumpled and stained, as though someone had wept bitter tears over it. It read:

THE ORBAN STORY
By Ruth Stevens

An infant rocked from birth in a cradle two hundred feet long! A little boy lost in a high-test rocket-ship, seesawing through space! Around and around he whirled, obeying instructions from the age of eight, eating just enough to keep the spark of life from going out.

No disease germs bothered him out there in space! There were no measles, whooping cough, scarlet fever, just instructions in his head and—a long forgetting!

What did he think about all those years? What did he dream about?

Phillip Orban was born on that ship. His father invented the Orban drive and built the first rocket-ship with an outer hull of sufficient hardness to withstand the stresses of a billion-mile journey through space.

But the power drive gave out and the ship never completed its journey. It went into a circular orbit in the Asteroid Belt and for seventeen years it drifted through space.

The boy's mother died when he was three, mercifully from a heart attack. The boy's father kept a log. We know that he climbed out on the naked hull when the boy was eight, to tighten a loosened gravity plate. A minor repair job—but he put off coming back. Put it off forever!

The boy remembered to remember. Food concentrates should be taken sparingly, twice a day. "You're seven now, son! No—eight tomorrow! Old enough to look after yourself!"

He hadn't one bitter-sweet, earthy moment to cling to. He'd never played pranks on other kids, or dressed up on Halloween, or gone fishing in a creek. He'd never watched the dawn redden a haystack or the moon silver the sea.

There were books on that ship. An odd assortment of books. The Old English Nursery Rhymes, Mother Goose, the Brothers Grimm, Lewis Carroll. And "How to Build It" books. How to build it if you were Michael Faraday or Edison or Steinmetz or Mullson. But Phillip Orban read every book on that ship. The psychologists who are in charge of him now won't tell us why they're so excited about his marginal notes.

They found the ship and Orban at last, sank magnetic grappling irons in the hull and towed it back to earth. They returned Orban to his home in North Dakota, the family home, within a dozen yards of his father's dust-choked workshop.

A boy of seventeen, watched night and day by three trained psychologists. A robust boy, physically almost a man, would have to be terribly warped not to resent that! They're studying him like a guinea pig in a cage. And here's one unladylike journalist who raises her voice in protest! If the Orban boy—

Wayne shuddered, folded the clipping and crammed it in his vest pocket.

Kenneth Wayne began remembering things: about a machine in an open field, spilling an eerie radiance! And Dr. Bryce struggling with the Orban boy in front of the machine, and plunging backwards into the light. What shocking, incredible event had taken the famed psychologist from the sunlight before he could regain his balance?

Wayne also remembered that the Orban boy had fled, taking the machine with him! A hue and cry had been raised in the nation's press. A shrill screaming, journalism raised to high C. Had Orban deliberately pushed Dr. Bryce into the machine?

If an individual were the sum total of his experiences from birth, would not the whole outlook of Orban depart from the human norm? It was a terrifying thought! Was Orban a malicious monster with an inhuman capacity for deceit? Was he—

Twang!

Wayne wheeled with a gasp of horror.

A barbed and deadly looking arrow was quivering in the wall directly opposite the machine! It was an arrow two feet in length —fitted with metallic feathers to give it steadiness of flight, and tipped with a point of jeweled brightness, visible through the translucent plastic of the wall.

Stark terror twisted Wayne's features into a glazed, unnatural mask. That the arrow had come out of the machine he could not doubt. It was directly in line with the "croquet wicket" and there was a spattering of blood on the still quivering shaft.

There was blood on the wall too! Yet Wayne was quite sure that the arrow hadn't grazed his flesh. Automatically he raised one hand to his cheek, and then stared at his palm. His hand gleamed whitely in the cold light. That dripping redness had come out of the machine along with the arrow! The arrow had missed him completely.

Whom had it wounded?

Wayne was swaying in sick horror when a knock sounded on the door and a familiar voice said:

"Ken! For heaven's sake, why did you lock the door?"

Wayne turned, unlocked the door and threw it open, his face white.

The girl who came into the room was vividly alive. Coppery hair she had, cut in a bang, and her lips were slightly parted, her cheeks flushed. She was plainly out of breath and a little angry to be barred by a locked door, after climbing two flights of stairs.

Ruth Stevens did not look like a newspaperwoman. She was striking in a challenging, vibrant way—the kind of girl who could change a man's center of gravity with a look, a quick smile.

She wasn't smiling now. Her eyes darted to the machine and then to the arrow.

"The Orban boy," Wayne said. His voice was thick and it trembled a little, as though he were just about to lose control of it. "He's here. You wrote an article about him, remember? Would you like to meet him?"

Ruth swayed.

Wayne thought perhaps she was going to faint. It was a crazy thing to do, but he leaped toward her without realizing that he was standing a yard from the machine.

As he caught her in his arms something caught him. It was like a fierce rush of wind. It was cyclonic. It whirled him around and started pulling him backwards, straight toward the machine. He held on to the girl without realizing that he was pulling her inexorably in the same direction.

Ruth screamed.

The room seemed to pinwheel. It was much easier for Wayne not to let go of the girl. He did not realize that she was in deadly danger. He thought only of protecting her. There was a howling in the room as light blazed out from the croquet wicket to envelop them.

Far off as though in an inverted lens Wayne saw the Orban boy rushing out of the kitchen, his bearded face twitching in terror. Then everything in the room seemed to whip away into emptiness. . . .

Stability came back in slow stages. Wayne was aware first of warmth in his arms, a cry quavering from human lips. Then of a firm surface taking shape beneath him.

He was sitting on the ground holding Ruth in his arms. She was struggling to free herself, one hand pushing against his chin, her face a blob of whiteness.

He was sitting with his back against a firm stone surface, staring down at her. He could see her face clearly now, distinct and white in a blue glimmering light.

"Ken, where are we?" she choked.

It wasn't an easy question to answer. It was a world of rugged contours. They seemed to be resting on a plain that sloped away into glowing blue mist. There was a curious, dynamic quality about the landscape. Its very emptiness thrust itself on Wayne like chords of music struck wildly on a piano.

Certainly he was resting with his back against a stone wall of some sort, rising sheer behind him. When he turned his head he could see the wall clearly.

With a little groan Ruth disentangled herself and slipped to the ground at his side, making it easier for him to take note of his surroundings.

There wasn't very much to take note of. Just the wall and the bleak, desolate landscape. A few pebbles were scattered about, and—something small and globular and blubbery that was stirring in a cuplike hollow directly in front of Wayne.

Ruth cried out suddenly and plucked at his sleeve.

"Ken, look! That little egg thing is alive!"

An egg thing! Of course, it did resemble an egg. It was veined and oddly cracked and something wet was spilling out of it. Something projected from it too—the long shaft of an arrow.

Wayne's neck hairs rose. He got up and staggered toward the "egg" and as he did so the whole surface of the wall swept into view. It bore an unmistakable resemblance to the Great Wall of China reduced to fairy-tale dimensions.

Rugged and battlemented it was, but small—not more than thirty feet in height at the tower sections and much lower in between. It curved in and out over the plain, under a sky of fiery blueness, to lose itself at the horizon's rim with a kind of downsweeping rush that conveyed an illusion of motion.

The egg-shaped object had stopped moving when Wayne dropped to one knee beside it. The arrow had pierced it cruelly and Wayne could not doubt that it had ceased to feel pain. The little white tadpole arms which sprouted from it were limp now, completely inert in the blue glare. Equally limp was its puckered, little-old-man face, the mouth hanging open, the heavily lidded eyes drained of all expression.

Wayne did not attempt to withdraw the arrow. Obviously the egg thing was dead. He was glad that it could not return his stare. He arose and turned to Ruth.

"It was alive!" he said. "A ghastly little animal with an almost human face, shaped like an egg. I can't believe—"

Twang!

As the arrow sped past Wayne he leaped back with a startled cry. Something huge and blue had come out from behind a bend in the wall to aim a bow at him. He caught a brief terrifying glimpse of it as it darted back into shadows.

Wayne turned abruptly, and gripped his companion's arm. "We've got to get away from here as quickly as possible," he whispered, with hoarse urgency.

"Away?" Ruth stared. "How can we? The machine has disappeared."

"We must get away from this wall. There's something deadly here that shoots to kill!"

"Human beings?"

"Man-shaped beings. Angular, flattish. They don't seem to have any heads."

Ruth swayed toward him. "Are you sure they're shooting at us?"

"We can't wait to find out. We've got to run for it."

"Where do you think we are?" Ruth breathed in sick horror. "Another dimension?"

Before Wayne could reply, another arrow sped past them with a vibrant twang.

They broke into a run, keeping close to the wall, their shadows preceding them in the blue glimmering. Panting, terrified, they came to a brief halt beneath a darkly looming tower that seemed to bulge out over the plain.

At right angles to the wall, a hundred feet from where they were standing, a vast circular mound bisected the plain, its edges misty in the strange light.

"Come on!" Wayne urged. "That mound may be hollow. We've got to chance it."

They were in motion again, racing toward the mound, when they heard a fluttering sound. It seemed to beat out from the mound in tangible waves, like the stirring of migratory birds gathering in great numbers in a tree and shaking the air with their flutterings.

Then up from the mound twenty or thirty winged black shapes soared, spiraling up into the sky in a wild, soaring ecstasy of flight. Almost instantly the arrows started flying.

One by one the birds dropped like dead sticks to the ground, amidst a flurry of deadly arrows. With hoarse cawings they dropped, their feathers flying, their long, lizardlike bodies pierced by the cruel shafts.

Back into the mound they dropped, straight down with their flutterings stilled.

For a moment there was complete stillness on the plain, unearthly, terrifying.

Then Wayne said in a choked voice: "Does all this remind you of something? In a vague, distorted, nightmarish way, I mean? Does it?"

Ruth stared across the plain before replying. It seemed to her that she saw shadows, angular, menacing, moving in the distance, on the rim of her vision. It seemed to her that she saw the shadows of bows, blue on the plain. "Humpty Dumpty sat on a wall!" she said. "Six and twenty blackbirds—baked into a pie!"

"You thought of that too, did you?" Wayne's lips were white. "We didn't see Humpty Dumpty fall, but it was a great fall he had. It smashed him, and not all the King's horses and all the King's men—"

"Stop it!" Ruth's voice was almost a scream. "There are no horses, no King's men here. That egg was a hideous little animal with the face of an ape. And blackbirds don't have lizardlike bodies."

A procession came around the mound with a far-off beating of tiny drums. It could not be said that they were King's horses or King's men. They were something not quite rational.

It was a winding procession of egg-things, tottering on little stumpy legs, and prancing green shapes that bore a startling resemblance to walking-stick insects. The eggs were linked together by dangling wisps of filmy stuff. When they came closer the filmy stuff resolved itself into a net, glimmering, metallic.

They're going to catch Humpty Dumpty when he falls, Wayne thought wildly.

Suddenly the long wall stirred with activity. A dozen little egg-shapes were running along it, dodging and weaving, their tadpole forelimbs quivering.

A shadow, dark, ominous, moved on the plain.

Twang!

The running eggs splintered as they fell. A wailing went up from the advancing procession, long-drawn, shrill. The "King's horses" swerved in closer to the wall, the net floating free.

Too late! The ground was littered with writhing and dying egg-shapes, shattered, spilling their yolks. One was not writhing. It was completely bashed in, a flattish horror swimming in its yolk.

Suddenly Ruth screamed, "Look over there! It's one of those angular, headless things. It's aiming at us!"

The blue bowman had stepped out from the shadow of the wall, and was sharply limned in the downslanting radiance. His arms and legs were metallic zigzags, his body an angular shaft. He was slim-waisted, broad-shouldered, a Zeus lightning bolt aping the human form, a cut-out shape like a figure on a lampshade, standing poised and vibrant as he raised his bow.

Wayne swung about, took hold of Ruth and dragged her to the ground. The arrow twanged horribly as it left the bow. They could feel death brushing them as the ghastly, headless figure sprang back into shadows.

Then they were in motion again. They headed straight for the mound, past the procession of toddling ovoids and prancing walking sticks, their faces livid with terror. Another arrow sped past them, raising a flurry of dust as it thudded into the base of the mound.

Then they were climbing up over a tumbled rampart of thrown-up earth, and down into a hollow rimmed with blue shadows that seemed to leap toward them out of the gloom.

"That took courage," a quiet voice said.

The man was sitting on a boulder with a Seral hand blaster cradled in his arms. He was a big man, with massive shoulders and a gaunt-featured face. He had torn off his shirt and made a bandage of it. He sat blinking against the light, his right arm wrapped in the bandage, his eyes deep pools of torment. Empty cartridges lay scattered about his feet.

He smiled wryly and started to rise, then thought better of it. "I'm James Bryce!" he said. "How did you get here?"

He gestured toward another boulder as he spoke. "Sit down, man. You're safe for the moment. I've been holding them off with carefully timed blasts."

Wayne helped Ruth to the boulder, and stood for an instant with his back to Bryce, breathing heavily as he stared across the plain. Then he swung about. Words poured from him, a torrent of words.

When he had finished Bryce nodded grimly. "I see! Pretty

gruesome from start to finish. We're trapped in a world we never dreamed existed, and—we've the Orban boy to thank for it!"

Ruth spoke then. "Mother Goose," she whispered. "The Old English Nursery Rhymes. A world that exists only in the Orban boy's mind. Somehow he's made it real, three-dimensional."

Bryce smiled oddly. "You've been thinking that? It's not true, but it does you credit. It means you have at least a toe-hold on reality. You know that reality can't be reshaped to any kind of preconceived mental pattern."

Bryce forced a crooked smile. "What would another dimension be like, logically? Peopled with men and women like ourselves? A mathematician's pipe dream?

"Rubbish, don't you think? Why should intelligence in another world function on a plane that's comprehensible to us? Take the dreams that have found their way into the literature of childhood. What is the literature of childhood? Isn't it, in its purest essence, a world of nightmare fantasy and diffuse cruelty, without rhyme or reason?"

He looked up quickly. "Humpty Dumpty sat on a wall, Humpty Dumpty had a great fall. What made him fall? Poor old Humpty Dumpty! Weep for him—rush to the wall and watch the poor, pitiful attempts that will be made to put him together again.

"Nothing cruel about poor old Humpty Dumpty. He'd tear your heart out. A lovely goofy old egg. Where's the cruelty then? I'll tell you. The picture that devilish fantasy conjures up is the essence of cruelty. A smashed, quivering, alive egg, in torment, scattered, spilling its yolk."

"But—"

Bryce waved a muscular hand. "The world of a child's reading is like a pack of tarot cards. You know the old stories of children bewitched and tormented by cruel goblins. There's a grotesquerie in it like nothing on earth.

"A child's mind is wide open to it—receptive. A child really sees into that world, in its dreams. Do you know why? That world really exists—as a sober scientific reality. When we grow up we forget to remember."

Bryce's lips tightened. "A child's mental receptivity isn't

blunted by the world around it. It grows up in two worlds at once, until it adjusts to our reality. But the author of the Mother Goose rhymes remembered his dreams of childhood more vividly than most men."

Bryce made a deprecatory gesture. "The real Humpty Dumpties are quite a bit different. Living ovoids who are always the victims of a cruel sport, destined to be shot down, and rescued too late by their little stricken fellows.

"There's a doom on all of them. What a weird, wild, shooting-gallery world this is! Sport, archery. The headless archers. They're cocks of the walk here, I think, swaggering, slim-waisted bullies. But there's something automatic about them. I don't think they're prime movers."

"I'm glad to know that," Wayne grunted grimly.

"The prime movers who created this world may be a kind of puppet master without visible substance. What impressed me from the instant I arrived here was the automatic, clockwork aspect of everything. It's intangible, hard to pin down. But a sensitive man can hardly fail to be aware of it."

"I know what you mean," Ruth whispered.

"Everything's cyclic. Those blackbirds ascend like clay pigeons released in swarms at intervals, and when the eggs fall, others take their places on the wall. We haven't penetrated very deeply into this world. Old Mother Hubbard may be here too, with a ravenous dog that isn't a dog, really.

"It may be a dog that keeps going to an empty hole in a cliff wall. He rushes in, barking furiously, and comes out without a bone. The cupboard is bare. Then an arrow pierces him, and he's a dead dog for a while. Jack and Jill go up a hill, a target for the headless archers.

"They're Jack and Jill in the Nursery Rhymes. Here they may be angular, metallic figures, but horribly vulnerable. The pail of water is shattered, spills and runs like quicksilver into the ground. Jack and Jill pick themselves up, pluck out the arrows and go staggering back up the hill to get some more water, their faces writhing in agony. Or maybe there are Jack-and-Jill replacements and the first pair die!"

Bryce's gaunt face was deadly pale now in the chill blue light.

"It's a hellish clock set in motion and staying in motion," he added.

"The Orban boy knew what this world was like," Wayne said, slowly. "He called the archers blue bowmen. How does he fit into it?"

"Remember his strange destiny!" Bryce answered. "That's the crux of it, man! He—"

Bryce stiffened in sudden wariness, tightening his grip on the blaster. "Here they come," he warned. "Keep your shoulders down. They converge, shooting with ugly deliberation. But blasting scatters them."

As he spoke three blue archers came into view between the wall and the mound. They emerged from shadows to stand motionless for an instant on the plain.

Sweat ran cold on Wayne's back. The upraised bows were trained on the mound, taut and glittering arcs of metal bisected by gleaming arrowheads. The shanks of the arrows were drawn back by hands like mailed fists, the bowstrings beaded with light.

The archers released their bows simultaneously. There was a single sound, like the crack of a whiplash in utter stillness.

It was followed by a dull roar. Smoke swirled from the mound as Bryce blasted, blotting the archers from view. When it cleared two of the original archers were lying prostrate, but their numbers had been augmented fivefold.

Bryce was cursing softly and holding on to his bandaged arm. "Caught an arrow when I came through," he muttered. "That concussion opened up the wound. Why did it have to be my right arm?"

"Here, let me take that!" Wayne said, wrenching at the blaster.

"I can handle it!" Bryce grunted, in angry protest. But Wayne had the blaster now and was aiming it at the headless figures, his lips a bowstring line.

Twang!

One arrow for an instant that seemed a lifetime, cleaving the air. Then came a dozen arrows, a hundred, in a swirl of brightness above Ruth's terror-wrenched face.

Wayne blasted not once, but four times in hot anger, his throat a throbbing ache. The energy flare blotted out the plain. A blinding pulsebeat seemed to throb in the heart of the blast, amidst an expanding whiteness.

When the smoke thinned out, the plain was littered with recumbent archers. A few were shattered. It was incredibly nerve-torturing to watch metallic zigzags twitch and pick themselves up, and whip away into shadows like seared leaves.

"That was reckless!" Bryce grunted. "A single blast would have stopped them just as effectively. They can't stand the shattering repercussions!"

Wayne sucked in his breath. For an instant he remained in a crouching attitude, his eyes bright with horror. Then he stood up. "I asked you how the Orban boy fitted into this," he said grimly. "Let's have the rest of it."

Bryce shrugged. "Consider, man. For generations kids have been brought up on a diet of fantasy and reality. One offsets the other. Children don't know how real the fantasy world is, and the reality around them quickly blots out Humpty Dumpty."

"Well?"

"The Orban boy knew how to read and the fantasy world took on an unnatural brilliance for him. It became his own intimate, private world. He had just the stars of space to look at and that inward vision. Don't you see? He had to get to it. He had to break through the dimensional barrier. It became an obsession with him."

"But how?"

"There were technical, scientific books on that ship. The Orban boy knew how to read and he wasn't an animal. He was whiplash smart. Even at eight, he had a working grasp of applied physics. He'd talked a lot with his father, knew how to tinker."

Bryce kicked at a loose stone with his toe. "Perfectly normal boys of eight have had I.Q.'s of one-fifty. Mozart was an accomplished musician at six—a great one at nine. Boy chess wizards crop up in every generation and chess is a three-way game. You've got to peg your naked intelligence into a background of semantics and applied psychology. But some kids get monumental backgrounds just by keeping their eyes and ears open.

"What do we know about human intelligence anyway? Illiterate rustics have mastered atomic theory, using hit-and-miss techniques. The Orban boy was precocious, granted. But we know even less about precocity than we do about adult intelligence."

Bryce looked at Wayne with a torturing surmise. "That kid slipped away from us for a couple of hours, got to his father's workshop. Sheer carelessness on our part. When I saw him with the machine, I rushed out of the house, and tried to reason with him. We got into an argument and I started tugging at him.

"Luckily I'd strapped a Seral blaster to my hip, just in case. But it was the blaster that got in my way. It weighed me down—in the wrong direction. When I tripped I didn't have a chance of regaining my balance."

Bryce shrugged grimly. "I've been holding the archers at bay ever since. Funny thing about that machine. It's light—weighs about eight pounds. Orban can carry it, but if you stand directly in front of it, your goose is cooked. After I came through I didn't see the machine. It must be invisible from this side!"

Wayne nodded. "We didn't see it either!"

"It's still around, I imagine. When I came through an archer saw me. I caught an arrow in my shoulder. I ripped it out and hurled it from me, and it vanished in a flash of light. You say you saw an arrow come out. Probably it was the same arrow."

Wayne started to speak, but Bryce stopped him. "Listen!" he warned.

From the purple-hollowed middle of the mound there arose a strange, mournful, dirgelike sound. Then up from the mound came a dozen "blackbirds," their lizardlike bodies quivering as they went spiraling into the sky.

No arrows pursued them. There was utter silence on the plain.

"Looks as though we've thrown a scare into the archers for the time being," Wayne muttered, but there was no exaltation in his voice.

Bryce shook his head. "They'll attack again," he said, with grim conviction. "Those birds were simply lucky this time. I wonder if they realize how lucky—or care!"

Ruth whispered: "Six and twenty blackbirds, baked into a pie!

When the pie was opened, the birds began to sing! My what a dainty dish, to set before a king!"

Her voice rose sharply. "Ken, who do you suppose the king was? We haven't seen him! Is there a king?"

"A symbolic embellishment," Bryce snapped. "I'll say it again: Mother Goose is simply this world seen through the distorted mirror of a child's imagination. The author of Mother Goose transformed what he saw here into a medieval fairy tale. We'll never see the king because we have nothing in common with him."

The sky seemed to darken as Bryce spoke. Wayne looked up in chill apprehension, a shudder coursing up his spine.

"Oh, no!" Ruth choked.

But there *was* something high in the sky, swinging slowly down toward the mound. Something globular that wore what looked like a shining crown and shook like a mound of jelly.

Nearer it came and nearer, swinging lower with each vibration of its circular bulk.

It blazed suddenly into sharp visibility. It wasn't a king, and it wore no crown. It was a floating spheroid, veined and translucent, filled with an intricate assortment of moving parts that gave off a continuous whirring sound.

A madness seemed to possess Wayne as he stared up at it. He cupped his hands and shouted: "Who are you?"

"Who are you?" came back in a staccato echo.

"Who are you?"

"Who are you?"

"If it says: 'Who am I?' I'll die!" Ruth screamed hysterically.

"Who am I?" the spheroid flung out. "I'll die!"

"Wait!" Bryce gripped Ruth's arm, his lips shaking. "It's a tropism—nothing more. A kind of echo response. You soft-pedaled the 'If it says'—then screamed the rest. It only picked up the last part. It didn't change the question. It simply repeats what it picks up!"

"No—it doesn't," Ruth groaned. "Now it's going to say: 'You'll die!' "

"Not unless you scream it first," Bryce said, with a brittle laugh. "Look, I'll show you."

He cupped his hands. "You're going to win through," he shouted.

"You're going to win through!" came back.

"It's a promise," Bryce shouted.

"It's a promise!"

"You see?" Bryce turned with a relieved grimace. "You seldom get a better answer than that. It's a regular politician's answer. What you want to hear comes back in a vibrant echo that means absolutely nothing."

The gear-and-wheel-filled spheroid was swinging back now, straight up into the sky. It dwindled rapidly, vibrating as it swept from view.

"Well, that was your 'king,'" Bryce said. "I've a hunch it's simply a weird regulatory mechanism that sweeps down at long intervals. A kind of cog in the clockwork setup—a stabilizing flying pendulum that's needed here to keep things moving on an even keel."

Ruth sprang back with a gasp of horror. Three tiny metallic shapes had scurried swiftly over the edge of the hollow and were descending into the blackbird pit with the blindly groping movements of terrified moles.

Moles? Why not mice? Blind mice?

Wayne was the first to say it. "Three blind mice, see how they run—" He stopped, appalled.

"Finish it," Bryce muttered. "They all ran up to the farmer's wife, who cut off their tails with a carving knife."

He gestured eloquently. "I told you cruelty was of the essence here. It's a savage, senseless, last-turn-of-the-screw kind of cruelty. Why mutilate blind mice? Isn't that utterly ghastly? And yet it's in Mother Goose.

"There's hardly a Mother Goose rhyme that doesn't shadow forth this world. The hunters and—the hunted. Creatures pursued by blind cruelty, shot down in flight. Who killed Cock Robin?"

A grim puzzlement seemed to grip Bryce. "Cock Robin! That's the cruelest one of all. It's so devilish in its wicked, eerie malice that some editors of Mother Goose omit it entirely, as not for children!"

He frowned. "Just who was Cock Robin anyway? Why was everyone so horrified? Cock Robin with his bleeding breast, the taut and quivering arrow. Why was Cock Robin so different, almost a stranger to this world? Why did the cruelty pause to wonder? Why did everyone answer: 'Not I! Not I!'

"Why did everyone single out Cock Robin as the one creature in this world who shouldn't have been killed at all?"

Bryce strode back and forth, glancing over the mound as if in chill apprehension.

"A curious thing! Not only the Mother Goose rhymes shadow forth this world. An ancient Chinese vase bears the inscription: 'See how the harsh blackbirds fly into the bronze sun, pursued by the arrows of darkness!'

"And Lewis Carroll! There are things in *Alice in Wonderland* that seem to shadow forth this world. Why was Alice so real to generations of children?"

He shrugged. "A few men remembered their childhood visions well, apparently. Too well for comfort. The Looking Glass was simply a symbol. You step through. The Orban boy got at the scientific reality behind the symbol. He actually constructed a dimension-dissolving looking glass!"

Ruth stared at him. "Are you claiming that all children are dangerous little monsters?"

Bryce shook his head. "No. Only very special children. Children who were cut off from all normal activity, as Orban was. Their visions spur them on. But I think we've always known, subconsciously, that a child with too much knowledge would be dangerous. Why do people like to make up rhymes about the wickedness of children? Remember the Little Willie rhymes:

'Little Willie hung his sister
She was dead before we missed her!
Willie's always up to tricks!
Ain't he cute? He's only six.'"

From somewhere on the plain came an answering whisper, as though the cruel words had goaded the blue world to activity again. A low rustling swept across the plain, ominous, mind-chilling.

"Here they come!" Bryce whispered, reaching for the blaster.

Wayne moved quickly to forestall him. He had the weapon and was leveling it before the psychologist could glower in protest.

A shadow fell on the plain, grew larger. The blue archers were stepping out from the wall with a deadly deliberation, their Zeus-taut bodies wrapped in a translucent glimmering.

Wayne held his fire until a dozen archers released their bows simultaneously. There was a pulsing at his temples as the trigger clicked. A swirl of whiteness followed the click, a silent whiteness for an instant as brief as a dropped heartbeat. Then a thunderous concussion shook the mound, hurling him backwards. . . .

An hour later Wayne sat with his back to the tumbled earth rampart, his face haggard with strain. A thin smoke was swirling over the mound, an acrid haze which obscured the slope directly below him and blotted out the crouching bulk of Bryce. But he could feel the despair which emanated from Bryce—a palpable force. Bryce spoke suddenly. "I'm glad we saved one blast!" he muttered. "We've got to decide how to use it!"

The words fell on a chill, deadly silence.

Then Ruth uttered a sobbing moan. Wayne knew with grim certainty that Bryce would not attempt to spare her. If he thought the blaster should be turned upon the hollow and held in steady hands, he would say so.

They sat silently together for an instant, not daring to voice what was in their minds.

Then Bryce spoke directly to Ruth. "By heaven, you're a pretty woman!"

A sudden, hot anger swept over Wayne like a flood of molten lava.

"If we had any chance at all," Bryce added, heavily, "Ken would have a rival!"

Wayne suddenly realized that Bryce had more delicacy than he had given him credit for. He had chosen an odd way to announce that there was no hope, but Wayne was glad that he had not phrased it brutally. His anger evaporated.

Twang!

The arrow sped in close, barely missing Wayne. The archers were in motion again. As they drew in toward the mound, their bows thrumming, the air grew thick with deadly arrows in flight.

There was a continuous, deadly twanging, a drumming in the air, a drumming in Wayne's skull—a reeling giddiness. Wayne did not hesitate or swing about to voice an agonized doubt. The suddenness of the attack had settled the issue for him.

The last blast would not be guided by another man's caution. His decision was made, and nothing could alter it.

Wayne blasted with a quick intake of his breath.

The spurting radiation struck the plain with a mighty roar. Wayne felt again the shattering recoil, the shoulder-bruising impact of a heavy weapon leaping in his clasp.

For an instant fire and smoke danced on the plain, swirling over the base of the mound and blotting the archers from view.

Then the smoke thinned, and rolled back over a seared expanse of desolation the more awful because it wasn't quite empty. One archer was still advancing, swaying a little as it climbed the slope through the dissolving smoke, its bow upraised.

The archer was almost at the crest of the mound when Wayne sprung straight at it. With a sickening twang the arrow left the bow and thudded into the earth rampart at Wayne's back. Then Wayne was beating with the blaster against the archer's angular body, swinging with it again and again, pounding with all his strength.

The plain rang with the harsh, strident clang of metal against metal, as though knights in a tourney were colliding head on in a suicidal contest of strength.

With a savageness that amazed him, Wayne fought the archer back down the slope. Eyes wild, lips quivering, he brought the sharp edge of his weapon against the horror's gleaming chest, and slashed downward at the low-slung metal quiver at its waist.

Strange how much courage a man had when his life was forfeit, strange the shining strength, like a shield around the heart, blazing out for all to see!

Arrows were spilling from the archer's quiver and its body was twisting strangely when something seemed to lift it up and hurl it backwards toward the wall. Wayne cried out hoarsely as the writhing horror receded from him, twisting and turning like a gale-lashed leaf. It vanished abruptly, in a blinding flash of light.

And as it vanished a running figure came into view on the plain.

"Orban!"

It was Ruth who shouted it, coming to her feet in wild disbelief. The Orban boy was running straight toward Wayne and waving his arms in urgent appeal.

Wayne couldn't catch what the Orban boy was shouting. But he could see that the running lad was gesturing him back toward the mound.

In a daze of fevered uncertainty Wayne swung about and started climbing. He heard himself sobbing. His legs threatened to give out, but he managed to gain the crest and fling himself down in the hollow. He lay on his stomach, staring over the rampart, his lungs choked with dust.

Slowly he became aware that Ruth had thrown herself down beside him and was clinging to him in sobbing relief.

The Orban boy came over the crest with his breath coming in choking gasps. He flung himself down directly opposite Wayne, and raised himself on one elbow.

"Had to wait—until I was sure I could get you out," he breathed. "That man—" He gestured toward Bryce. "He's not so important, but you're my friend! Had to save you, Ken!"

Wayne stared, his mouth strangely dry.

"My idea was to hide the machine until I was equipped to come into this world, Ken." Orban went on feverishly. "I worked something out, but it wasn't good enough to protect me in here. That's why I asked you to help me hide the machine!"

"Just what did you work out?" Bryce asked. His face was ashen, but his voice was firm enough.

"Just met Ken last night," the Orban boy wheezed, his eyes

shining. "But he's the only friend I ever had. He was going to hide me. That's more than you'd do, I bet."

"You're right about that," Bryce said, with a harsh laugh. "I asked you, What did you work out?"

For reply the Orban boy opened his hand. The object which rested on his palm was small, no larger than a jackknife. It was shaped like a compass. Six tiny glowing knobs projected from it, but otherwise it was unbelievably makeshift in aspect, as though the Orban boy had walked into a toyshop, picked up a compass, and twisted two wires intricately around the floating needle. And now he was displaying his prize with a fierce pride, as though he'd done something remarkable.

"Worked hard at it, in Ken's kitchen," the Orban boy explained. "Took me six hours to get it right."

"You're sure it works now?"

"You bet I'm sure," Orban said, pridefully. "The segments which feed that loop have been moved around, see? They pass right under the contact points. All I have to do is draw the second loop into position by the attraction of the needle."

As he spoke the Orban boy pressed one of the little knobs on the rim of the "compass." The "compass" lighted up.

"Now it's ready!" Orban said.

Bryce stared. "Ready for what?"

The Orban boy cupped his palm over the "compass."

"You'll see. Watch!"

Light from the "compass" streamed out between the Orban boy's fingers and haloed his entire hand. Slowly he raised his hand and turned to Wayne with a triumphant cry.

"Look at what is happening!"

It was impossible not to look. The blue world was in sudden, furious activity. Down from the sky the "King" wobbled, to hang directly over the mound. The blind mice ran backwards out of the blackbird pit and six and twenty blackbirds rose into the sky. And out on the plain stepped a dozen blue archers, their bows upraised.

But the most terrifying thing was the gulf which yawned suddenly on the plain. Out of it stumbled something that looked like a jigsaw giant, bent nearly double. The figure went reeling and stumbling over the plain, as if in unendurable agony.

The figure was metallic, very similar to the archers, but it moved in a dizzyingly crooked way that brought a tortured reeling to Wayne's mind.

"'There was a crooked man and he ran a crooked mile,'" Ruth heard herself screaming.

Twang!

An arrow pierced the blueness, thudding into the shoulders of the crazily weaving figure. The giant stumbled and fell forward, its loose-jointed arms flailing the air. It dragged itself crookedly backwards toward the trapdoor in the plain, its movements still geometrically insane.

Suddenly the archers froze. They stood rigid, unmoving, their bows held at grotesque angles. The "King" stopped vibrating. It hung motionless above the mound, congealed into the blueness like an ice-frozen jellyfish.

Every other object within view took on an aspect of rigidity. All movement ceased. There was a stillness so absolute, even the stirring of a blind mouse would have set up a din. But the mice were stiff, rigid, impaled in a web of stillness.

"By heaven, he's stopped the clock!"

Bryce's stunned cry shattered the human stillness on the mound. But the "King" did not echo back the sound, and nothing on the plain moved.

Orban grinned then, for the first time. "I knew it would work," he exulted. "It had to work. It'll all start up again, in just about three minutes. Can't stop it for long. You've got to get out fast."

"You mean," Bryce wet his shaking lips. "That little thing–" He waved one arm "–stopped *all that?*"

"Size hasn't a thing to do with power," the Orban boy said, as though he were addressing a child. "Shucks, I could blow up every city on earth–big cities like New York and Chicago–with something half the size of this!"

Ruth swayed.

"I fixed the machine so you can see it from this side," Orban said. "When you go out, I'll break it up from this side. Come on,

Ken. You got to get around that wall before it all starts up again."

All four of them started off, in the direction Orban indicated, running at top speed.

Nerve-torturing thoughts, that fitted no pattern of sanity or logic, were churning about at the back of Wayne's mind, as he dashed after the youth. They rounded the wall in a run, the Orban boy in the lead, Bryce bringing up the rear.

The wall hadn't changed, but the toppled Humpty Dumpties resembled eggs that had dropped from a cold-storage crate. Their tadpole arms had ceased to jerk and their spilled yolks were frozen solid.

The Orban boy paused an instant to nudge an egg with his toe. "The poor little thing!" he murmured, shaking his head. Then he was in motion again.

When the machine swept into view, the Orban boy was breathing heavily, his face tight with strain. But he kept on running until he was directly in front of it. Then he turned and waited for the others to come up.

"I can't go with you, Ken," he said, when Wayne reached his side. "I belong here. Always have—always will!"

He shuffled his feet as he spoke and suddenly, he was thrusting out his hand.

Wayne stared at him in stunned horror. "But you can't remain!" he protested. "When those devilish archers start up again—"

Orban shook his head, squinting back at the wall. "I don't dare leave, Ken! Know what would happen if I did? I'd get careless and there'd be more accidents. People would get killed—everybody on earth, maybe. I know so much in some ways—I'm not safe to be trusted!"

The Orban boy was behind the machine, and he was rushing straight toward Ken with the machine held out before him.

It was a little like passing into a warm shower. The light was all around Wayne, lashing against him, before he realized that he was no longer on the plain.

"Good-bye, Ken!" came in a dwindling echo of sound. "Sure was great to have a friend!"

Wayne picked himself up from the floor and looked around him. He wasn't alone in the room. Ruth was sitting beside him. Bryce lay on the floor, and the croquet wicket was dwindling to a shapeless lump of metal in a dwindling blaze of light.

Bryce was getting slowly to his feet, and staring about him with fiercely contracted brows, as though he despised Wayne's taste in furnishings and was about to say so.

Bryce went to a chair and sat down. "Nice place you have here, Ken," he said.

Suddenly his composure broke. Sweat came out on his face, the back of his hands. He shuddered.

"He'll never come back," he whispered. "We've seen the last of him."

Wayne got up and staggered back against the wall and stared at Bryce.

Bryce made a despairing gesture. "I wish now I'd said a few kind words to him. It was the least I could have done."

"Why?" Wayne was hardly aware that he had spoken.

"Oh, it's a paradox, all right," Bryce murmured. "Just like—the paradox of time travel. Say a man lives now and goes into the past. Doesn't that mean he's always existed in the past? But how can he go back to where he's always been?"

Ruth had gotten up and was staring at Bryce with startled eyes. "What has that to do with the Orban boy?" she asked.

"Say you went into another dimension today," Bryce said, slowly. "Say it was a kind of timeless dimension—from our point of view. Wouldn't you in a sense exist in that other world from the very creation of that world? Wouldn't you freeze into that world and become a part of it from the start?

"If someone from our world saw that other world centuries ago, wouldn't he find you there? I think he would."

Bryce paused an instant to stare out the window of Wayne's living room. The murk of an October morning stretched beyond the pane. He stared at Wayne, then at Ruth, as though challenging them to deny that they had just returned from a quite different world.

"You saw that King-clock horror, swinging down from the sky!"

he went on. "A mechanical tropism enabled it to echo back sound. Suppose a boy, who never should have gone into that world, was trapped in it. Suppose he shouted his defiance to the sky as the arrows sped toward him.

"Suppose he shouted his name, in anger and fierce pride, recklessly as a defiant boy might well be tempted to do. His name, now and forever, long before he was born into our world, our time, because he'd made himself a timeless part of that timeless world."

"Well?" Wayne's voice was a puzzled whisper.

"A good many boys have nicknames. Young Orban's given name was Phillip, but his father didn't call him that."

Ruth gave a cry. "No! Oh, no!"

"Suppose the King-clock merely repeated the name," Bryce said gently. "Suppose the boy lay slain on the plain and the King repeated his name, over and over. And the little lad who was to write Mother Goose saw that world in a dream of childhood and heard the name. The author of Mother Goose must have been an imaginative child.

"Remember—he saw the horror only dimly. It bore the name of a familiar bird. Why not a bird lying slain on the plain and everyone in that world asking: 'Who killed Cock Robin? Not I? Not I?' Everyone horrified, appalled, because Cock Robin was a stranger in that world."

"You mean—"

"It was an intangible thing, the uniqueness of Cock Robin, but it must have communicated itself to the author of Mother Goose. He imagined the rest, the protesting voices, the shared horror, and remorse. He made a fantastic little nursery rhyme about it."

Bryce looked at Ruth. "Do you know who Cock Robin was now?" he asked.

Ruth drew closer to Wayne before she spoke, as though she dared not remain alone with such a burden of horror and pity resting its cold weight on her heart.

"His father called him Robin!" she whispered. "Robin! Robin! The Orban boy—he was Cock Robin!"

BETTYANN

Kris Neville

"Bettyann" is something of an underground classic of science fiction. Connoisseurs often cite this rich, moving, sensitive story of a girl who is not quite human, speaking of it as one of the finest versions of its theme, but hardly anyone seems actually to have read it—chiefly because its appearances over the years have been in obscure collections quickly vanishing from sale. Perhaps restoring this famous but elusive story to print in this volume will solve the problem for a while.

Kris Neville is a Californian whose first science-fiction stories were published in 1949. His work includes such favorites as "Take Two Quiggies," "Closing Time," and "Old Man Henderson," as well as a sequel to "Bettyann" called "Bettyann's Children," which appeared in 1973.

It began to spit snow, and the car skidded slightly on the wet pavement.

"Please drive a little slower," the woman said, and the baby began to fret.

The man glanced at the luminous watch dial. "We've got to hurry," he said.

"They'll wait," the woman said. "Hush," she said softly to the baby.

The man bent forward slightly, his eyes staring out into the darkness. Snow splattered against the windshield to be smeared away by the fast-ticking windshield wiper.

"They'll think something's happened to us, and they'll go on," he said.

"No, they won't," she said. She petted the baby.

The man slowed the car for an upward curve that bent around a dripping cliff.

"What does the mileage gauge say?" he asked.

"Ten thousand, one hundred and . . . nine," the woman said, reading slowly by the dim dashlight.

"In about ten miles, then, we better start looking for the cutoff."

"We've got nearly half an hour, so please slow down," she said.

Reluctantly he eased up the footfeed.

The baby cried restlessly.

"She's in the body nicely," the woman said. "She wears it better than we do."

"We'll have trouble getting her out," he said. "It's all she knows."

They were silent for a moment, and the tires sizzled. Then the woman said, "Did you enjoy it?"

"It was interesting. Very pretty little world. Absorbing greens, I should say."

"There was one nice sunset."

"The planet near Elsini is better for sunsets: remember the one in which the cloud formations . . . ?"

"*Please* drive slower, dear! It makes me nervous."

Annoyed, he looked again at his watch.

"We've got plenty of time," she said.

"It's quite a distance down the cutoff. It's nearly a mile, remember, to that awful-looking white house; and they're far enough beyond so the ship will be out of sight."

The woman fondled the baby. "It's a nice planet, in its way; not all hard, not all soft. . . . She's actually growing in this body, have you noticed? She's gained several pounds, I imagine. Just look how fat her arms are!"

"After all, it's the only one she knows."

"Dear! This car is awkward on a road like this. So . . ."

"We're almost to the cutoff."

"Look out! Look out!" she screamed in terror.

It was a truck. It was jackknifed across the pavement. The car rushed up the steep grade to meet it. And the headlights of the car patterned briefly the outline of the truck driver, lying on his back on the wet concrete, tinkering with one of the multiple-tired rear wheels.

The driver of the car slammed in the brake pedal. The woman gasped. And the car swayed sickeningly. It leaped to the shoulder of the road, flashed by the stalled truck, and continued up the grade. The man fought the steering wheel, struggling to wrench the car back onto the pavement. The front wheels locked in a rut. Grunting explosively, the man jerked the steering wheel savagely to the left; it slipped from his hands, and the still hurtling car was free. The car leaped and bounced and teetered for an infinite second and crashed down sideways. It turned over and over until it half bent around a thick cedar tree nearly twenty yards down the slope. It lay quiet with one of its front wheels spinning leisurely.

The man had fallen across the woman; neither body moved; and slowly, second by second, life bled away, and the two bodies crumbled inward and dissolved, and all that was left was fine grayish powder.

Up on the road, the truck driver, white-faced, waved his flashlight beam in the direction of the wreck. For a long moment he heard nothing but the monotonous drip of water from a tree across the road.

Then he heard, very distinctly, a baby crying.

For a long time after the accident, for an eternity after the accident, Bettyann (although that was not yet her name) knew a puzzling progression of hands and faces and lights and shadows. At first, and for half her life and more than half, there had been a great, unlocalized pain. She cried whenever a nurse brushed her upper left side, but she could not associate the terrifying pain with the nurse's act, or ever quite understand the fear that came with a certain footstep.

At first the hands that touched her seemed no nearer than the far and dimly seen walls. Things existed, but they had no relation to each other and none to her.

Objects first began to order themselves when she became aware that the addition of something to her lips produced the cessation of a sharp, painlike pang not at her lips. Later, she found that the wall of the crib arrested the motion of her fist. And after that, as knowledge of space, bit by bit, became a part of her, she was acutely aware of the increasing rhythm of light and darkness.

Later still, she was able to localize the great pain, but by then it was not nearly so severe. It was in the left side of her body and eventually in the region of her left shoulder. Involuntarily, muscles seemed to want to exercise a second arm there; but the arm did not respond; it lay inert. One day she realized that the fist of the arm was tightly clenched. She tried to flex the fingers, but they would not flex. She cried herself to sleep.

Time began to move faster after she was transferred from the hospital to the State Home for Orphan Children, but the months were still long, because each was still so large a part of her total existence. At length there came the day when her routine of feeding, exercise, and sleep was broken by strange perfume and by new, quiet voices in kind-toned gabble, and soft, gentle hands. The hands most of all were pleasant.

"Isn't she a darling little girl?" the woman said, and the man agreed, and the nurse said, "Her arm was injured in an accident. She'll never have the use of it." And the man and woman murmured sympathetically.

Later, although Bettyann could not know this, the man and woman spoke with the gray-haired lady superintendent; and after that, they went away to think over all the implications of adopting a child with only one good arm.

The car in which Bettyann had been found lay rusting in a scrap heap. The dust on the seat was gone as thoroughly as yesterday's sunlight. The investigation of the accident was closed. And stranger things had happened before and will happen again in the memory of man than a demolished car and a deserted baby.

The soft hands remained in Bettyann's memory, and, vaguely discontent, she wanted them to return.

When finally the hands did return (and Bettyann was now her name), she gurgled happily, and upon being lifted, she kicked her feet in excitement.

Solemnly, as though Bettyann could understand the words, the superintendent said, "This is your new mother, Bettyann. Momma Jane and Daddy Dave."

And because she was pleased, Bettyann told them what the nurse who fed her always said: "Da da."

The woman blinked her eyes, looking down at the infant, and said, "Would you like to go home with us, Bettyann?" And the man cleared his throat.

The superintendent's eyes sparkled, and she smiled almost enviously. "I'm sure she'll be the kind of a daughter you deserve, Mrs. Seldon."

"Of course she will!" Mr. Seldon said. "And smart! She just said da da, didn't she? She's as smart as a tree full of owls already."

His wife said, "At first we'd half planned on a child a little older. In fact, we weren't even sure we wanted a girl at all. Until we saw Bettyann."

After more words, equally unintelligible to her, Bettyann felt a blanket being wrapped tightly over her body, and after that she felt bright sunshine on her face and then a sickening forward movement and strange noises. Soon the movement became mixed completely with the sound and everything was a hurrying purr except for the bobbing green tassel from Mother Jane's bonnet and the drowsy murmur of Daddy Dave's voice.

Jane studied Bettyann's fist with minute attention, and Bettyann liked the feeling of the warm palm around her hand.

"They're awfully small, the fingers," Jane said.

"Let's see," he said, glancing over quickly. "Hummm. They are, at that. When we get home, you know, we'll have to get a birthday cake for her. I forgot it."

"Isn't she a little young for that?"

"I wouldn't say so, no. I'm sure I had one, my first birthday. I had a cake every birthday. When I went to college, my great-aunt, Amelia, sent me a cake my freshman year, as I remember, and she'd wrapped up nineteen little candles in waxed paper and laid them right on top. Of course she'll have to have a cake."

Watching Bettyann, Jane said, "I think I'd rather not know her real birthday."

"Eh? And why not?"

"To make it the day we take her home, that makes it seem as if she's just been drifting around somewhere, waiting for us to come along."

Dave muttered happily to himself.

After a moment, she said, "Dave, dear. You don't really suppose the parents *will* turn up?"

"Of course they won't turn up!" he snapped, suddenly almost angry. "What the devil should they turn up for? After running off and leaving her in the wreck like that!"

"That's what I think, too. But you're not worried?"

He puffed his cheeks. "Even if they did, how could they get her back? What difference would it make?"

Bettyann was five, and it was her last spring before school, and she sat at the window staring longingly into the forbidden yard. She and Jane had had a postbreakfast clash about the toy doll. ("Bettyann, you simply must *not* leave your toys scattered about where someone's liable to stumble over them.") It was at least the tenth offense in the last two months, and Jane, at last becoming angry, had punished her.

All morning she sat at the window pensive and sad, and lunch eaten, she resumed her post. Her patience was rewarded when finally, relenting, as Bettyann intended she should, the severity of the confinement, Jane said, her voice slightly amused, "Very well. You may go outside now."

Bettyann slipped from the chair, her lips tucked into determined resistance. She went to the door without a word, and through it, proudly, into the sunshine. She was stubbornly indignant, and her childish jaw was set with unshakable resolve. She went directly from the porch, through the small cherry orchard, to the wealth of hollyhocks along the alley fence. She found a bee upon the lip of one of the flowers, a stunted plant within her reach, and with scarcely an instant's hesitation, she scooped up the bee and imprisoned it in her good right hand. She knew that Momma Jane would feel very sorry when she got stung. Daddy Dave, were he home, would chuckle not unkindly at the sting and say, "It'll feel better when it quits hurting"—his favorite statement for greeting her, oh so important scratches and bruises, a statement which infuriated her only to make her laugh through angry tears. But Momma Jane, seeing the savage hurt, would run to her and say, "Now, dear," kissing it, "let Mother put something on the nasty old pain right away."

The bee, when it finally stung her, hurt much worse than she had imagined it would, and she slapped her hand desperately against her dress to rid herself of the uncooperative insect. Then she ran toward the house crying, "I got stung! I got stung by a bee!"

The kitchen window faced the alley fence, and Jane stood beside it, waiting for her. She had her hands firmly planted on her hips, and when Bettyann rushed into the kitchen, she said, calmly, "I saw you deliberately pick up that bee, dear."

Bettyann blinked her eyes in surprise. "You did?"

"I most certainly did."

When she came to realize that the expected sympathy would not be forthcoming, Bettyann said, "I wish I hadn't, now." She left the kitchen and went to her room, and after crying a bit in frustration, she saw the humor of the situation, and she laughed about it, and eventually the bee sting stopped hurting.

Once more during the final, preschool summer, she received a bee sting, quite accidentally, this time. It was promptly administered to. And aside from the bees, of course, the summer was a pleasant one, and when fall finally came, as, she felt, it well might not have, Bettyann knew a touch of genuine sadness. Her question of the previous winter returned to puzzle her: Why must everything die in wintertime when we need the live greenness most of all? But as summer continued to fade away with quiet inevitability, she began to look forward, half fearful, half excited, to the new mystery into which she was shortly to be initiated.

On the first day, Jane walked with her to a foreboding white rock building from which she remembered having heard pleasant laughter the previous spring, and there introduced her to a not at all terrifying person who was to be her teacher for a whole, long year. She felt momentary fear, after Jane had gone, at being in a strange room, surrounded by strange and possibly hostile faces. She felt, for the briefest moment, as if she had broken away entirely from the certain security of the familiar home; the flower bed, the garden, the weathered oak, all solid and real, now seemed in memory, substanceless. She wanted desperately to rush after Momma Jane and run with her down the tree-lined walk, hurrying as fast as her feet would go, because the flower bed, the garden, and the weathered oak might not be there if she waited one endless hour. (Aunt Bessie had said to Momma Jane, "That's when you first begin to lose them. They're never quite the same after that. The teachers manage to take them away from you." To which Daddy Dave had said, "Nonsense, Bessie. She is, after all, only five." "But then, I suppose," Aunt Bessie had said, "it won't seem quite so bad for *you*, Jane, dear, as it would for—for, well you know . . ." At which Momma Jane's face had turned very red. And Bettyann had wanted to ask why that should be.)

After the initial shock of adjustment, Bettyann found the strange faces around her to be friendly. The first, bashful smiles of acquaintance came to be smiles of pleased recognition. Days began to hurry toward Christmas. And then, all at once, the holidays had come and gone, and bright, washed faces told with excited tongues of wonderful gifts from Santa Claus. And because there were so many new things to be done, it seemed that in no time at all sweet, lazy spring was back.

Just three weeks before school was dismissed, Miss Collier, the teacher, distributed finger-painting sets. "You'll get to play with sets like these all next year," she explained. And within fifteen minutes, she was standing over Bettyann's desk. Bettyann was working excitedly with brilliant colors on large, heavy paper. "What do you think your picture looks like, Bettyann? Is it supposed to be a big, brown cow or what?" Still working, Bettyann said, "It's a man in a tree." "Oh?" "Yes," Bettyann said, wrinkling her forehead, "the tree bark's all crum'led up, and the man's face is all crum'led up—right in the bark." "How very odd," Miss Collier said. "It looks as if you really painted it in, once I look for it." "I did." "No, child: I meant on purpose." "It *was* on purpose," Bettyann insisted, and Miss Collier laughed, rumpling her hair. "You should be a painter, then." After Miss Collier had gone, Bettyann, disappointed at being misunderstood, drew her fingers through the man in the tree and began to fashion the figure of a little girl. She tried to make the little girl's face seem as though you were looking at it from two directions at once.

During the final week of the school year, Miss Collier gave the children a series of simple aptitude tests. (Miss Collier was a recent college graduate.) Bettyann understood that the results would be very important throughout all the eight grades, so she tried as hard as she could. Later, when the principal was congratulating Miss Collier on her efficiency, while wondering what, exactly, should be done with the results of it, Miss Collier said, "This one, here, on Bettyann Seldon. She's certainly very intelligent, but I couldn't help feeling that the tests weren't getting at her real abilities; she seemed only half tested. I made a note about it on her form." "Oh, yes, I see," said the principal. "Of course," Miss Collier said, "I only had three units of elementary testing." And the principal, who had had none, remarked, uncomfortably, that he was sure it would be all very helpful and that he couldn't expect, after all, his teachers to know everything.

Bettyann was in the second grade for less than a month when one of her crayon pictures ("Almost good enough to be the work of an eighth grader") was posted on the big bulletin board in the main hall. Of another of her drawings, however, a semi-exploded view of a house with displaced hedge and chimney and furniture floating around the walls, her teacher said, "A little too unreal." And Bettyann resolved to be more careful in the future, for she did not want to be misunderstood.

She found the very elementary reading baffling until, midway through the year, she quit trying to associate the words with the pictures in the reader and began associating them with speech: and after that, reading was easy. She found in the group games and for ball passing in particular, that, with increasing familiarity, the shriveled arm presented scarcely any handicap.

But during the last part of that year and all of the next, her third, she came more and more to feel estranged from her classmates, and to a lesser degree, from her teachers, and even, but to a lesser degree still, from her parents. In class she came to fear that at any moment an unfortunate remark would elicit spasms of laughter; and at home she felt that there were things neither Jane nor Dave could understand, not in the way she understood, no matter how they might try, and failing to understand would, if she spoke of them, misunderstand not the thing itself but her for speaking. She withdrew inch by inch and became silent when others laughed and hesitant when others spoke boldly. ("She's a shy and sensitive child.")

Beginning her fourth year of school, no more than a week after the first session, one late autumn afternoon it was, when for the first parent-teachers' meeting, class was dismissed early and still unreacquainted children lingered in the schoolyard. Bettyann saw one of the older girls, a seventh or eighth grader, run from the empty teeters, kicking up white sand with flying tennis shoes, toward a vacant classroom, and she cried silently as she ran. Bettyann could see no reason for her action: the girl had been some distance from the nearest child. In that moment, Bettyann learned, and it was feeling more than thought, a second of certain insight, that each person was unique unto himself, and the memory of the tearful face told her that each, to his own degree, is misunderstood; and she, perhaps no more alone than the older girl, no more misunderstood than all the rest.

She was to have the same lesson repeated once more before she became a fifth grader. The second incident occurred not at school but while the class, under the supervision of Mrs. Fox, the eighth-grade teacher, who, Bettyann knew, went off to herself for a few minutes upon arrival to smoke a forbidden cigarette, was on a tour of the zoo some eighteen miles away in Joplin. The class went from Mark Twain School in a chartered bus, each child but Elmer carrying lunch in a brown paper bag. (Elmer carried a grown-up lunch box.) Within the park, for it was called a park rather than a zoo, there were many strange and wonderful and exciting animals. And when the eager class stopped beside the kangaroo, Willie, one of the smaller, less well-dressed boys, said, "Look! Bettyann's got a *kangaroo's* arm!" Bettyann, puzzled, looked at the kangaroo, frowned momentarily, and answered, "No, the kangaroo's arms are both all right; there's nothing wrong with either of them." Then she realized that the comparison was not based upon physical similarity. There had been resentment in Willie's voice, and viciousness, too. She knew of no offense that she had given him. She could not remember even speaking to him more than once or twice for he sat across the room from her and usually played by himself during recess. There was certainly no one-to-one cause-and-effect relationship. And, in thinking the incident over later, she wondered how it might be generalized in a picture of human relations: a group of people, perhaps, in pairs, each member of the pair chained to all the rest, with everyone pulling against the chains in an attempt to get closer to his partner.

She was supposed to skip the fifth grade; Dave, however, would not permit it. "She started school early as it is." And Jane agreed after the first excitement of her pride passed: "It wouldn't be fair for her to be almost two years younger than the others when she gets to high school." "And college," Dave added proudly. The parents nodded, and Dave held Bettyann on his lap and said, "She's as smart as a tree full of owls," and Jane said, "Be careful, Dave, or she'll grow too big for her britches." Dave said, "Nonsense. It gives her self-confidence."

All during her fifth year in school Bettyann made a special effort to accept the occasional strangeness of her playmates, to understand, as nearly as she could, their attitudes, and to adopt those attitudes for her own. At first it required conscious effort; later, it became automatic; and, as the school year drew to an end, she thought much as her playmates thought.

Spring came and then summer. And alone, one hot afternoon, she went to the flock of English sparrows on the lawn before the house and picked one up, gently, in her hand and held it to her face and cheeped to it. Dave came out, letting the screen door slam, and the birds flew in terror, and Dave said, "How the devil did you manage to slip up that close to them, Bettyann?" Laughing, she answered, "I just did." It occurred to her, then, to ask the question of herself; but there was no answer other than the one she had given. "I must have just been thinking right," she amplified, and Dave snorted, "Damned sparrows'll have the whole country some day." She turned to watch the sparrows fly from their tree limbs to settle a safe distance away in the dust of the driveway. And watching them fly, it seemed that she could, if she only knew how, join them and be as free to sail the skies as they. For an instant she knew great longing, longing to be released from the narrow, confining space of her world; to float, as the song said, where the south winds rise; to be, as the birds. . . . And the feeling passed: she was content. Here, around her, the quiet, sleepy afternoon. . . . She smiled, thinking of the light restrictions on her life: dishes to do, for which, of course, she was paid; "helping around the house," Dave's inclusive phrase that meant very little; attending the long, sleepy Sunday school, which Jane said, "won't do any harm. . . ." No, here in the hot afternoon she was free; and here, with the beat of town life around her, exciting, she was happy, and she was at a loss to understand the vast longing of a moment before.

The summer was unusually dry and she played outside a great deal, went to one wiener roast, attended a blanket party at Doris Heisten's house seven miles out in the country, and spent one week with Aunt Bessie at Lakeside. When the rains finally came they came in torrents that made the yard a welter of mud and the outside an extremely unattractive place: the rains flattened the dying hollyhocks, and later the first day, savage hail sheared leaves and twigs from the cherry trees and broke the glass front out of Al's Grocery across the street. She located *David Copperfield* in Dave's haphazard collection of books. There were perhaps twenty volumes in all, some left over from college, some purchased during a half year of enlightenment when he was a member of The Book-of-the-Month Club. She was attracted by the name, a copperfield, in her imagination, being an endless stretch of copper stalks glistening in the sunlight, row on row, like tall corn. It took her several days of conscientious reading to finish the book, and all the while, for sleepy background, the rain drummed deliciously on the roof and dripped from the eaves and moved upon the windowpanes. She did not understand all of it, but she laughed with Mr. Micawber and cried when Dora died. And when the book was done, she felt glad and proud, although she could not understand why she should. It was a strange book, and unreal. But unreal in a different way than *Alice in Wonderland*, which she had read twice, each time feeling that she was missing something of the utmost importance.

Time hung poised with the rain, but finally sunny skies came and school and winter and then always-exciting spring again. But this spring, before her eighth year of school, was not the same as the ones that had gone before. The adults were quiet and waiting; and they seemed about to bubble over with some unexpected excitement. In early May the excitement broke, and the war in Europe was over. Everyone cheered and cried and was happy. But beneath that, Bettyann felt, sad and still, a little guilty perhaps because the war had eaten deep into men's hearts and burned there like a horrible conscience. Just before school began again, the other war, too, ended, and the people were deeply frightened at the way it had happened. But peace was a vast relief, and without fully knowing of war, Bettyann cried when she heard the news.

Bettyann's grade school teachers all agreed that she was not quite like the rest of the children. ("All *I* know," Mrs. Fox said, "is that she had an absolutely phenomenal grasp of historical time.") And her difference, whatever it was, was not altogether reflected in her superior grades. It was deeper than that, deeper, even, than her conduct: for she played as the others played, recited much as they recited but with occasional flashes of adult perspective, teased other girls about boy friends but was never teased in return, passed notes surreptitiously in class, and blushed whenever she was caught chewing gum. The deep difference, in the final analysis, it must have seemed to the teachers, was that she should be quiet and pensive and reserved, and that she completely refused to be.

As everyone expected, she graduated from the eighth grade at the top of her class. And then, during the prehigh school vacation, the frightening biological change came, and she became hurt and puzzled, and for the second time she withdrew into herself. (It was that summer that Jane and Dave told her of the adoption: and they attributed her new reserve as much to that as to anything else.)

The sense of having been unfairly imprisoned by nature, of having been tied in some vague way against her will to a new and not altogether likable body, persisted into her freshman year. There were flashes of acute embarrassment, not for any act, but, in surprising moments, perhaps while reciting at her desk, for existence itself. And always it seemed that just beneath the borderline of consciousness there lay a way for her to escape from everything that oppressed her.

Her art, so hopefully displayed and marveled at in grade school, no longer interested her; ambition lay dormant. Waiting, she instinctively realized, to be released by more knowledge and to be given direction by increased insight; and some day, in full maturation, many things would be possible for her; but not now. She was listless at her books; school bored her. She half wanted, more in daydream fantasy than anything else, to become a . . . an airplane pilot—or explorer—or gambler—or race car driver—or something else in revolt against this weak, feminine body. (Dave jokingly said, "A girl ought to know what she wants to be by the time she's in high school," and she answered, genuinely concerned, "I wish I did; I wish I did.")

The year wore on exasperatingly. Until, one day in late November (but almost a month beforehand!), the boy who sat across from her in general science class, Bill Northway, asked her to the holiday freshman prom, and she came home enthusiastic to announce: "I've got to learn to dance!"

Dave received the news with the false surprise of elevated eyebrows, and for a moment she was afraid he would refuse her request. But he nodded his head and said gravely, too gravely, "We'll have to see about it," which, she knew, meant, "Yes." The next Saturday afternoon, with a three o'clock appointment, she went to Zobel's Studio For The Dance. The studio was no more than one room above a bar, just off the Square, and the music was from a portable phonograph and scratchy fox trot records. Often the fox trots were only dimly heard above the stentorian bellow of the jukebox below. Mr. Zobel, a slender, effeminate man, had one assistant, a willowy blonde, Mrs. Hawkins, who danced with the older boys, those who objected to dancing with Mr. Zobel. It was the only studio in town, and Mr. Zobel taught tap and ballet as well as ballroom, and rumor said that he once danced in night clubs in the West and had a movie contract until something happened that led immediately to his return to his parents' home and the subsequent establishment of the studio. Bettyann had pliant movements, and she molded easily to Mr. Zobel's discreet lead, and after two private lessons, dancing, with an uncanny ability to anticipate his steps, became as natural for her as walking. And after the holiday prom, she was happy again, and reconciled to the no longer quite so new body.

Social science, as the elementary course in government was called, was first to prick her awakening interest, early in the second semester, and she began to read, avidly, the front page of the newspaper and ask puzzled questions, all of which, to the best of his ability, Dave tried to answer, and, when she appeared unduly depressed at some of the information, he quieted her with, "After all, honey, we don't live in the best of all possible worlds; it's just the best we have."

She checked out the two books on government from the school library, and, in further search in the public library, came across, quite accidentally, while browsing through the three hundreds (the assistant librarian had forgotten it was not to be filed in the stacks open to the public) *Das Kapital.* Miss Stemy, the librarian, said when Bettyann brought the book to the desk, "Aren't you a little young for such heavy reading, Bettyann? Wouldn't you like better an adventure novel or something like that?" But Bettyann said, "I'd like this, Miss Stemy, if you don't mind," and Miss Stemy, who was an old friend of the family and very fond of Bettyann, said, "Of course, my dear, if you wish it." And later she phoned Dave to say, "I thought you might like to know your daughter is taking up *Das Kapital.*" "She is, is she? She's a curious little devil, all right," Dave said. "Then you don't mind my letting her have it?" "Oh, I don't think it'll completely corrupt her mind," Dave said, "but please, Lee, if she comes in after Krafft-Ebing, don't let her have that. Not until her next birthday, at any rate."

Bettyann understood very little of *Das Kapital;* but the *Communist Manifesto* at the end of the book made her blood sing with enthusiasm. She felt she could do something for the workers immediately, and she went to Dave, who, after listening tolerantly to her excited speech, agreed that a sense of indignation at social injustice is invaluable, but, unfortunately, due to the absence of a revolutionary movement at the moment which had the people's welfare at heart, he was afraid there was very little one small girl could do; and that she'd have to content herself with such unexciting but necessary jobs as helping with the next Red Cross and Community Chest campaigns.

During the summer her enthusiasm for social science waned. By the beginning of the second year, she had taken up with almost crusading zeal the pursuit of a new occupation. She was determined to become a doctor, or failing that, a nurse. She talked it over with Dave. Dave agreed that it was a worthwhile career and that it had many rewards. "But you've got lots of time to decide," he said, reversing, it seemed to Bettyann, his previous stand. And Jane, seeing her idealism, encouraged it soberly, but with equal restraint. Neither of them wanted to see the idealism expand unnaturally to the point where the world would crush it, and, disillusioned by asking too much, make Bettyann cynical and hard in automatic response.

"There's so much to do!" Bettyann cried. "So much that *needs* being done!" Dave said, "But it takes a long time and a hot oven even to hatch an ostrich egg." And Bettyann laughed, wanting to say, Of course, I know that. Dave said, "Society, I'm afraid, is pretty complex. Things that look simple frequently aren't." "Being a doctor's simple," Bettyann said. And Jane said, "It all depends on the kind of person you are."

She began to draw again, mostly pen-and-ink sketches,

carefully, painstakingly wrought, but this time the drawings were abstract and personal, devoid of meaning for any save herself, and she burned them after they were completed. She could feel the growth of power, the technical mastery of line and perspective, a growth that would some day, when she was ready, permit her to do pictures that would say something to others as well, and something important, too, which, as yet, she had only the merest inkling of. She made the beginning tries at reading poetry (she liked best Emily Dickinson), and she discovered the adult short story in the O. Henry award volumes. She located them neatly arranged in dusty rows by the south window of the public library. The stories seemed to say a great deal about life, but it did not seem possible to put what was said in words other than the authors'. And society, she began to realize, *was* complex, and again she was lost and uncertain.

"Silly, romantic little fool!" she told herself, when she let her emotions be caught up and involved in something beyond her immediate life. She saw a picture of the Great Pyramid, and she was overcome by the grandeur of human effort and the sad, defiant presumption of a forgotten man, and she wanted to write poetry about the great ebb and swell of human life, something like Sandburg's *The People, Yes.* (She had read an excerpt from it, and the title haunted her, and later, when she learned that Hamilton called the people "the beast" she could not help thinking, Yes, but the people, yes!)

Toward spring of her second year, at the fourth all-school assembly in the auditorium after the holidays, the principal announced, to her complete surprise (she had been carrying on a whispered conversation with Bill Northway seated beside her), that she had been selected by the faculty as the Outstanding Sophomore and would be sent, all expenses paid, by the Federated Women's Clubs on a one-day trip to Jefferson City, the state capital, next Friday.

Friday came quickly. And she found herself in Jefferson City admiring Thomas Hart Benton's murals and Carthage Marble. She had tea in the Governor's Mansion and actually talked for a few moments, alone, with the governor's wife, an embarrassed sparrow of a woman who seemed flattered that Bettyann should notice her to say: "It must be tiresome to have so many strangers in your house like this," to which the governor's wife replied with an almost defeated sigh, "It is, sometimes, my dear," and then brightly, as if it were amusing and yet important, "Did you know the high school groups are the worst about the silverware? We lose thirty or forty spoons every time." Bettyann laughed and said, "I must take a spoon, then, mustn't I, to avoid being different?" So, conspiratorially, the governor's wife went to the table where the lemon ice was being served and took a silver spoon, wrapped it in a paper napkin, and carried it back to Bettyann. "Don't let them see you," she whispered. "Of course they wouldn't *say* anything. Votes, you know. But it's always best not to let them see you."

After that, the school year closed explosively, and Bettyann, over Jane's halfhearted opposition, got a job in Scot's Five & Ten, where, for nearly three months, she waited on and came to know the townspeople. And as she came to know them, all of them, the petty and haggling, the self-consciously magnanimous over a dropped penny, the aggressive, the shy, the bold, the frightened, she knew that there was an infinite variety, and that very little was constant except, perhaps, the expression deep in their eyes, and nothing was certain but the multiplicity of ambitions, hopes, fears, desires.

There was much not to be forgotten: "Whistling" Red, a wizened man (a retired farmer, an ex-bootlegger, a renegade Catholic priest: there were many stories about his unknown past occupation) who whistled tunelessly to himself wherever he went and who attended every funeral and always cried into a big linen handkerchief. "I go for the music," he confided to Bettyann. And Ed Barnett, who fell four stories from the Drake Hotel to the sidewalk and walked away without even a bruise. And William Seiner, who shaved his head every Monday because he was afraid of dandruff. And Miss Leonard, who, it was said, got mad when her sister married, and stayed in bed for twenty years out of pique. She was a prim old maid with bright brown eyes, and she chuckled when she told Bettyann, "Get a man, child," winking, "get a *man*."

There were these, "Whistling" Red, Ed Barnett, William Seiner, and Miss Leonard, and a hundred more besides; and the days were warm and happy. Bill took her several times to the movies and once skating and twice swimming. And there were dates with other boys, and one of them, one evening, quoted a great deal of the poetry of a man named Swinburne: the boy looked very soulful when he quoted it, and she wanted to laugh, but she was too polite.

In her junior year she had to write fiction for the English class. In her first composition, she used what she thought to be a new style for description. But as the teacher pointed out, in such passages as "Creeping moonlight genuflected at gaslight shadows, writhing," the style rather got in the way of the thought, making the whole more meaningless than necessary; and she agreed. (Always, at every turn, in painting, with prose, in conversation, there was the difficulty communicating.)

"Look at the yard," she said to Bill, while the two of them sat on her quiet front-porch swing, "and tell me what you see."

"Well, let's see," he said, pretending seriousness, as he frequently did, without, she knew, ever taking her seriously. "There's the grass. Yes, that. And there's the moonlight, of course. And the shadows from the old oak tree, and then there's the sidewalk with cracks in it, and the hedge. . . ."

Bettyann wanted to explain that one might, in addition to seeing the physical details, see also the relation between them, or one of the many relations between them, that caused everything to be ordered into a pattern. "There's first of all aliveness and deadness," she said. "Look how they're balanced against each other. See how soft the aliveness is and how hard the deadness is. Look at the aliveness of the grass and the oak; and the deadness of the sidewalk and the shadows. See how the leaves seem to suck at the moonlight and how the tree bark lies inert before it."

"Hummm," Bill said, only half serious, now, and then, no longer pretending, turned to her with catching laughter to say, "You've got a pretty head full of stars."

She knew that he did not understand. Or, more accurately, perhaps, he heard the words, understood the meaning, but did not feel as she felt the essential rightness and truth of them. But he did sympathize with her; he did not laugh coldly, but in friendship, and that made everything quite all right.

During the summer before her senior year, Bill went east to see his mother, who was divorced and lived in New York City, and, when Bettyann saw him again in early autumn, he was old and wise with travel, and deliciously she knew that she had been waiting for him.

The final year of high school opened, and together she and Bill went to the movies and walked the quiet streets and drank Cokes in Gray-Reynold's Drugstore and laughed between classes. And his lean face was handsome.

But that he was soon to be drafted cast a net of dizzying uncertainty around their every handclasp and knit them together even as it promised to shear them apart. She wished desperately that this fact of divorcement might suddenly vanish. She wished—what nonsense she knew, even in the dream of it—that she might some way serve in his stead; or that a quick illness would come and pass and leave him with her to nurse back to health. Her other daydreams were quiet and contented and vaguely maternal; and surely, she thought, in close living, day to day, he will come to understand me as I must be understood.

Then, as spring came again and his draft date drew nearer, their lives became more desperate and frantic until, one evening, she knew with sudden insight that her dream was splintering. Her eyes were distant and angry and she was hurt and she reached out desperately after him, making, in memory, a perfect little idiot of herself and pushing him even further from her. Finally, to her shame, she cried bitterly and unfairly, "You've got to have a woman with *two* arms, haven't you?" and the dream lay at her feet, ruined forever, and even in the instant, the hot instant of the words, she knew that, for the first time, she had used her handicap to try to win advantage and that she could never again make that same mistake. And after he had gone, she remained weeping on the porch swing in hurt repentance, and mortification.

Sadness came in; she could never be happy again; resigned, never happy. As she sat in the darkness, staring out at the stars, she felt wave after wave of longing.

The world around her, silent, was quietly sad, and the air was quietly sad, and the leaves dripped quiet sadness; and life, too, was sad.

The first week afterward was endless: in her mind, a sad, blue tune, low, minor, coloring her movements and humming behind her ordinary conversations.

Two weeks later still, three weeks to the day since Bill had left, left although daily she saw his faraway face in school, Dave called her into the living room and said without preamble: "How would you like to go to Smith next year?" She was stunned for a moment, and Dave explained that Lee Stemy, an alumna of Smith, herself, had been looking forward for the last several years to getting her a scholarship; and in view of her remarkable high school record and Miss Stemy's influence the scholarship was practically assured.

Bettyann's first thought was for Dave and Jane, and she tried stumblingly to argue that it would be unfair, after doing so much for her already, for them to give her the money for a school in the East; but Dave insisted quietly that she should go, and eventually when Jane said, "We've saved a little here and there for you to go to college on," she agreed, conditional upon the scholarship and she felt proud and excited and happy, and it was fully fifteen minutes before she remembered that the world was a sad place.

Riding down on the train from Kansas City (she had flown there from Boston), a slow milk train that seemed to stop at every farm, Bettyann tried without success to sleep; and staring out the window, finally resigned to wakefulness, she slowly became aware of the extent to which less than one semester at Smith had changed the familiar countryside for her. When the train shrieked into a tiny depot, she could not help but notice the sense of isolation, the deadness, and the insularity of the station house and the somnolent main street.

Behind her in the East lay a different world. It was too new yet to be understood; but it was rich with promise like the sunrise. She caught glimpses of far horizons. New ideas from all directions, upon all subjects, were like keys unlocking doors to unexplored but exciting rooms, leaving her small and frustrated.

Her deeply hidden, latent talents were stirring under the impact. The promise of maturity was within her. Excitement trembled at her: at her fingertips lay an answer, and she could almost, but not quite, trace its outlines.

What am I to do with, how am I to fit into, this sad-funny world? What must I understand in order to be understood: and beyond that, in understanding, what then must I do? I wish I knew; I wish I knew.

And it was almost there on her mind's edge, almost, the answer. For one moment of utter loneliness (beyond the creeping train lay even, snow-splotched fields) she wanted most of all—as if that *were* the answer—to be completely understood. But that, she thought, would require complete identity; no, it is not that; the only one who can ever understand me completely is myself.

How can I fit into this sad-funny life: what is my role: what best can I do? The answer would be complex, as many-sided as life seemed, itself, to be, without easy definition. But this she knew, that she would be required to give unto them, the people, yes, of which she was a part and not a part, of her best talent so that, in return, they would give unto her that which she most needed. What did they want from her; what did she want from them? (I wish I knew; I wish I knew.)

And role, even that, was not enough. Beyond there was something more; perhaps some obscure branch of philosophy that she had never heard of dealt with that. Unless it was all on a purely local level, and need, where life and death seem senseless but through compulsive repetition gain meaning, need was the whole foundation: from complexity, vitality; from vitality, complex need: when the need dies, so, too, life: sleep, quiet, boredom, death. Role might be all. Could it be, she wondered, that beyond the role, I am always to seek because I have to, never to find because I cannot?

The answer, the lesser answer, trembled on her mind's edge, how can I fit into this sad-funny world? Not yet.

Someday, someday, someday, clicked the wheels.

And soon, sounded the whistle, soon.

Dave met her at the station, helped her from the coach, took her single bag. The air was crisp and wintry as they walked across the gravel, upon which snow had perished, to the waiting car.

Dave was silent after the greetings, and in sudden terror, feeling the strangeness between them, Bettyann cried, "There's something wrong!"

Helping her into the car, Dave said, "What makes you say that?"

"You're so . . ." She paused, seeking a word that expressed her conviction; seeking to name, for herself as well as for him, the quality from which the conviction sprang. A twitch of his mouth; the inflection of his greeting; the reservation she thought she saw behind his eyes? Not these; not entirely. It was as if she had heard, at the first moment, his secret thought, and now she could not remember it. In sudden panic she said, "Is Mom all right? Has something happened to her?"

Dave said, "Of course she's all right." He closed her door and came around the front of the car to the driver's side, and, getting in, said, "They've been giving you enough to eat? You certainly look healthy, but, I mean, you're getting *enough?*"

She laughed. "All I want."

"I went to the State University, you know. I was afraid in a private school maybe you wouldn't get enough. But it's good to see you. You look all right. . . . It's nice having you back."

"I was a little homesick," Bettyann admitted.

"How long do you have?" He set the cold motor snarling.

"Ten days."

"That doesn't seem very long. But you really like school? And what's it like to go to a big Eastern college? How are the other girls; do you have any trouble getting along with them? And . . ."

"Goodness! Not so fast! I've got ten days, Dad. If I tell you about everything now, I won't have anything to talk about tomorrow. Tomorrow I'll just have to be like some stick-in-the-mud of a farmer: 'Well, mighty cold today; looks like more snow; guess maybe the cold snap'll be pretty hard on the winter wheat.'"

The car made a U-turn away from the station.

She snuggled into the seat. "It's very exciting," she said. "It's different, too, than I imagined it." She paused to get her general impressions of Smith into words, and the silence, almost immediately, was uncomfortable. Puzzled by the feeling, she glanced out the window and said, "The courthouse looks cleaner."

"Didn't Jane write about that? They sand-blasted it last September. Just after you left."

"No. . . . She must have forgotten. . . . And what happened to Starke's Hardware Store? Isn't that a new front?"

"He sold the store. . . . They had a fire in the South End of town last month. It burned down the Castle Place."

"Mom wrote about the fire."

Dave turned right on Fifth toward Garrison.

She looked at him again. She tried to determine how to break through the hidden barrier newly between them. To forestall silence, she said, "It seems smaller. The town. More compressed . . . The houses aren't like New England houses. New England houses are all so old. They've been lived in so long that some of the aliveness has worn off on them. Our houses aren't like that."

Then to avoid giving the impression that because of three months in the East she was beginning to feel superior to the town, she said quickly, "But I guess, if you go out West, they're different out there, too. From pictures I've seen, you get an impression of isolated hostility. . . ." She bit her lip in annoyance, for the words seemed to increase rather than reduce the impression she had sought to dispel. She fell silent.

He drove to Maple; there he turned left.

The sense that something was wrong made Bettyann feel unsure of herself. She was half afraid to speak again for fear that the words would worsen the unknown difficulty.

"Is it something I've done or haven't done?" she said.

"What, honey? Haven't done what?"

"I *know* something's bothering you. I can feel it. Is it something I've done? Is it costing you too much money to keep me in school? If it's that . . ."

"It's nothing. It's . . ." Dave puffed his cheeks, a sign, Bettyann knew, that he was angry with himself. "All right," he said lamely.

"Ever since you were so high you could see right through me, I guess . . . I promised Jane I wouldn't tell you."

"Oh, Lord!" she said. "I'm sure it's nothing so very solemn. I can't imagine anything that has to be kept a deep dark secret."

He seemed more relaxed now that the barrier was down. "It's probably not solemn at all. Jane just didn't want to tell you until you were ready to go back. . . . There was a man here to see you. He was from Boston or some place back East. Jane was afraid he might spoil your Christmas; and she's looked forward to it so much. So she asked him if he'd mind waiting until you went back to Smith and see you there . . ." Dave had bounced the car up the driveway into the front yard. He cut the motor.

Bettyann was puzzled and excited too. She could not quite understand the excitement. "What did he want?" she asked, and her voice surprisingly was tense.

"I'll get your bag," Dave said. "Don't mention what I told you. I'd better tell Jane first. He wanted to tell you—he had some information about—it was something about your . . . real parents. He didn't tell us very much."

Bettyann's heart was pounding.

"Don't say anything about it to Jane until I talk to her," Dave said.

And then Bettyann was running toward the porch where Jane was waiting. Jane caught her, laughing, and she cried, "It's wonderful to be home, Mom!"

He came two days after she returned to Smith. She had been waiting with mounting suspense, and, when the house mother knocked on the door to say, "Bettyann? There's a young gentleman downstairs to see you. His name is Don Talley," she felt her heart jump violently.

"Don . . . Talley," she said slowly, letting the strange name melt into her mind. She did not like the name exactly. It was not the sort of name she had expected, and she wondered what face would go with it. "All right, Mrs. Reeves. Tell him I'll be right down."

As the house mother's footsteps sounded on the stairs, her roommate said, "Amherst?"

Bettyann shook her head uncertainly.

"Aggies? Williams?"

"I . . . don't think so."

"Well," the roommate said, disappointment in her voice. "Is he at least handsome?"

"I'm sure I don't know."

The roommate drew in her chin with amazement. "My God, you can't even tell whether he's *cute* or not?"

". . . I've never seen him before."

"And he's never seen you?" The roommate considered Bettyann's headshake. She blinked her eyes. "Now that I call real sex appeal: You've *got* it."

Bettyann smiled thinly.

"Gee, I wish. . . . Well, don't stand there. Go on down. Don't keep him waiting. Don't give the others a chance at him."

"I'm . . . going," Bettyann said.

"And you might ask him if he's got a friend who goes to Amherst or . . . Why, you're *white!* What's wrong? Are you scared?"

"No . . . Well, maybe I am, too, in a way."

"Are you in some kind of trouble? Can I help, Bettyann? Is there anything I can do?"

"I'm not in trouble . . . I guess I better go on down."

She left the room, and the door closed softly behind her. She walked down the wide stairs.

The crystal chandelier was tinkling musically. It had been moved by the wind when the huge, white door to the porch was last opened.

Bettyann stopped at the bottom of the stairs.

"He's the young gentleman talking to Mildred," Mrs. Reeves said when she saw Bettyann staring around the room. "He looks like a very nice young man."

"Yes," Bettyann said. "Thank you."

Bettyann crossed the room to where he was seated before the fireplace. Across the table from him, the brown-eyed Mildred was smiling with studied interest. Her hands lay quietly submissive in her lap; her lips were half parted.

When Bettyann reached his side he stood up and she felt a wave of uncanny recognition cross her mind. It seemed to come from outside herself.

"I'm Bettyann, Mr. Talley," she said.

"Bettyann . . . ah . . . Seldon?"

". . . Yes . . ."

Mildred leaned forward, her eyes aggressive. "Won't you join us? Don was just telling me he's from out West."

The fire threw a ruddy glare over his face. The face was still sharp from the cold outside; it was classically handsome, self-reliant, calm. Snowflakes glistened on his overcoat.

"Oh, Don, Don," Mildred said, standing and coming to his elbow. "Here," she said possessively, "let me take your overcoat, Don."

"No . . . Please . . . Don't bother . . ."

"I don't want you to think our house isn't hospitable. Let me help you off with it." She fluttered at his collar. "I want you to feel perfectly at home here."

"Really, thank you, no," he said with a trace of annoyance in his voice.

"But . . ."

"I prefer to leave it on."

Bettyann looked at Mildred's suddenly lax face; childhood, sad childhood, perhaps, gleamed through on it for an instant, and then Mildred recovered her brittle defense and trying to keep injury from her voice, she said flippantly, "I—oh— Oh, well. I can see you two want to talk."

"If you don't mind," Don said.

"Not at all," Mildred said pleasantly and distantly. After a moment she said, "I have a damned test in Lit tomorrow and I have to be studying in a minute anyway."

When she was gone Don said, "She came over and sat down in front of me and started to play solitaire on this table. When I didn't say anything she looked up and said, 'I major in sociology.' When I didn't say anything, she said, 'When I graduate I'm going down to New York and hang out a red light and do firsthand research. Where do you come from?' So I told her I come from the West. She got my name from that woman over there, I think."

Bettyann said gravely, and her eyes were puzzled, "I thought you told my parents you came from somewhere around here."

He nodded at the fire. "It was convenient to say that." He turned to her. "Can you leave this building now?"

"I–I could, I guess, if I wanted to." For the first time she noticed that he had an accent; it was not heavy, scarcely noticeable, and she could not remember having ever heard one quite like it before.

"I want you to get your coat. I want you to come with me."

The curtness of the statements made her want to answer an abrupt "No." But she held the refusal for there was something in his face–some indefinable tension–some almost sadness: some quality that drew her sympathy and excused his rudeness.

"Look at me," he said. "I have some things I must tell you about yourself. Look at me. Will you come?"

She looked into his eyes. She felt her heart flutter at the expression there. "I'll come." She reached out and touched his hand. "About my parents?"

"And about other things. Bettyann, I have a great deal to tell you."

"I'll get my coat."

"Please do."

He was waiting at the door when she came back downstairs.

Mrs. Reeves nodded to her and said maternally, "Don't forget, dear. Eleven o'clock."

Wordlessly, Don opened the door, and the two of them stepped out from the bright warmth into the dark cold.

"Where are we going?"

"To the Draper."

Her feelings toward him were confused. She did not altogether like him; she felt that she should not trust him as fully as she seemed inclined to. And yet, beyond that, she felt a kinship with him that she could not define. ". . . they won't let me go up to any of the rooms," she said.

"Walk by the desk naturally. It will be all right."

She thrust her face into the snow. She should, perhaps, be afraid, but she was not. Or perhaps she was afraid—not of him but that he might tell her things she did not want to know about herself. They walked past the chapel. (Snow creaked under their feet.) They left the white campus. They turned onto the main street, and downtown Northampton lay before them.

Her teeth chattered, and she held on to his arm.

Neon lights made the drifting snow soft orange, and their breath was frosty, and they heard laughter from a bar. They walked on. The town was readying for sleep.

At the Draper they stamped their feet free of clinging snow.

"Come. They won't notice you."

They walked up the outer steps, past the desk, and the drowsy clerk stared through her without interest, as if she were not there at all, and she looked at Don, whose face was relaxed.

Group voices, singing, drifted up from the Pilgrim's Room below. A girl laughed.

They walked up the worn carpet of the stairs leading from the lobby to the second floor. Don led the way to the room. He tapped lightly on the door. "Don," he said.

"Come in."

He opened the door and let Bettyann enter before him. He closed the door.

"Sit down, Bettyann," said the man on the bed. His face was old and lined and his eyes were deep set and his lips were thin and his hair was white.

She studied his face. "Why—why," she said in wonder. "*You're* not old!"

The man on the bed nodded.

"She's one of us," he said.

"You may call me Robin," the man on the bed said. "I'm going to tell you some very strange things, Bettyann."

Bettyann's eyes were wide.

"Don't be afraid."

Although her heart was beating wildly she said, "I'm not . . . afraid." And she wondered if that was strictly true.

Robin said, "Will you close your eyes, my dear?"

And his voice, like Don's, was a foreign voice; and beyond that, more than his voice was foreign. His face, everything about him, unreal. She could not pinpoint the unreality any more than she could explain how she knew that he was not old, any more than she could explain the feeling of kinship with him. She closed her eyes. Her lips moved silently. She stood upon the brink of something completely beyond all her experience. She waited.

"Listen carefully," Robin said. "Do you hear my thoughts?"

After a moment she breathed a tired sigh. "Yes." Inside her mind, not a part of it—terrifyingly, an intrusion upon it—she could feel words form and dissolve. They were indistinct and scattered, and beyond them there was an awareness of his presence. She felt revulsion, and she tried to fight against the words, but they continued, and then, after a moment, the revulsion passed.

"It is difficult to project this language. The symbols are too . . . heavy; not heavy, but . . . There's no word for it, here; *oxu,* in Fbun. You will see. You will learn many languages. Relax, my dear. I want to show you something more. Are you relaxed?"

"Yes," she said, but her body was tense.

"Try to follow this if you can. It may be difficult at first, so you must help me."

It was not words inside her mind, now, although she was aware of his presence. He was trying to guide her own thoughts. She put her hand to her forehead. He was making her . . . Her thoughts were . . . tugging . . . at a closed compartment, a new part of her mind, so strange a part that she tried to draw away from it, but he insisted . . .

"You must help," he said.

She moaned, finally, when she felt a sensation that was entirely different from any she had felt before: something like an electric shock, something like a fresh breeze, something like remembered pain.

"It's . . . it's . . . growing! I can feel it growing!" she cried.

She opened her eyes and looked at her left arm. She turned the hand over and over, holding it before her face. She felt of it uncertainly. "It's new," she said. "My arm is new." She turned her eyes, pleading, toward Robin. She wanted to cry; she felt tears well toward her eyes, and, with effort she blinked them back. Her skin prickled. "*Who are you?*"

Some part of her mind insisted, querulously, that this could not be happening. (Most real of all were the walls of the room: splotched wallpaper was so very stolid and prosaic that it shrieked refutation, but its presence insisted reality.) And the fingers of her new left hand, slim, delicate fingers, flexed in impossible freedom.

Robin stood and walked to the window. "You'll have to learn," he said. "Show her, Don."

Again she looked at Don. Instantly she felt her vague dislike dissolve into awe. She wanted to look away, to tremble, to, to . . . but she stood mute before him, unbelieving, overpowered, and her feelings, her thoughts, her whole body, were suspended in dull wonder. Slowly, before her eyes, he shimmered and changed. And after a moment he was not human.

"Oh!" she said, and her voice was weak and small.

"That's what we're like," Robin said. "That's what you're like, Bettyann."

"I'm like that?" she said. Don—what had been Don—was strange, compelling, not beautiful, but attractive in strangeness. She shuddered, scarcely able to think; to imagine that she, too, was like that was not to be believed, not in the moment, and belief and disbelief did not exist: merely wonder, mute.

"You'll get used to it," Robin said. "You will learn to take many shapes, to be, if you wish, something else: a bird, perhaps, an animal, or things with which you are not yet familiar. Once you learn you may take many forms."

She looked down at the new arm. Almost afraid to try to think, she let her mind explore the new compartment of its own accord. What happened seemed automatic reflex. Slowly the arm shrank to its original, withered shape. "Like that?" she said dully. "Like that?"

"You'll learn, Bettyann," Robin said.

Her heart seemed ready to burst. The very real—the oh, so real—walls of the room blurred, and the pattern of the wallpaper ran together, making her head ache with dry excitement. She expected them to crumble and resolve, the walls, into flowing, rippling lines that would merge away in all directions leaving her alone on a little island of solid carpet surrounded by moving silence. "Where are you from?"

"The stars."

". . . the . . . stars . . ." she said. Odd words. She had seen stars at night. They were very far away (but sometimes they seemed farther away than at other times). Tensions were building up inside of her body. The stars. It would be very difficult to control the tensions, and she was going to be whipped back and forth in her mind, thoughts pulling this way and then that, for some time. (Eventually, her mind would quiet: she could sense that, but it was meaningless for now there was no quiet.) It would take time. For the stars were very far away.

"We are not from this planet. Surely, you, yourself, Bettyann, must have felt that you did not . . . entirely belong to this planet. Surely you must have seen that you were different from the rest."

She shook her head, feeling the curls move, and one dropped over her forehead, and she brushed it away. Different? Different? "Tell . . . tell me about it," she said. Tell me very slowly, she wanted to say, a little bit at a time, for I do not fully believe you, yet, and I would not like to hear more that I cannot believe, except slowly, so I can fit in pieces (like in a jigsaw puzzle). I remember a jigsaw Jane and I worked: it was a picture of two dogs, bird dogs, and we had lost the box top, and it was a very long time before we could imagine what the picture was about. (Jane at first thought it was a behemoth, and I thought it was a grizzly bear.)

"There's a great deal to tell," Robin said.

Bettyann thought of the bird dogs, and, when Dave came home, he laughed and said, "Sure. It was on the box top." (And then she and Jane remembered, of course, and they said they'd really known it all along, now that he reminded them.) It seemed, suddenly, as if she had known forever: that here, finally, here were her people, people who could understand her as no one else had ever understood her, and she wanted to cry out with happiness, and then, not with happiness, but just surprise.

"We travel," Robin said. ". . . originally we came from a world that I suppose may have been much like this one. Our records show it was called Amio. We were already travelers when the race on this planet was still in its caves. It has been so long that our own planet is lost beyond the expanding horizon, perhaps twirls around a dead sun: I do not know. It has been very long. Our history . . . much of it . . . is forgotten. Who knows but perhaps all races pass through the same stages, and we may have been once like these new people among whom you have lived? But we travel now. We grew old . . . and wise on Amio, and after a long time, somehow, one of us discovered the *zeiui* effect, and we traveled far from Amio. And now we find a sunset here and the blue of waters a million-million miles away . . ."

As she listened the unshocked part of her mind realized that he was old, but not old in the sense she had used the word before, not as Earthmen are old; and it almost seemed as if his words were weary with age. The thought fluttered and died.

"When we came last to this planet," Robin said, "your parents were killed in an accident. I, myself, heard your father's thoughts just before he died, for I was waiting in a scout ship for him. I thought that you, too, were dead. . . . We returned a month ago. One of us thought he felt your presence on the planet. I was able to remember where the accident occurred; we computed the date from the Big Ship's log; we checked the files of a newspaper in the town nearest the accident. We found, indeed, that you had survived. From that, discreet inquiry led us to you."

". . . go on . . ."

"There are not many of us any more; not as many as we might prefer. It would be nice to have a new face again among us. There is ample room for you. And we have come for you, for you are one of us; we could not leave you here, lonely. We have come to ask you to come back to your own people, to travel with us. For you are one of us." He turned to stare out the window into the falling snow. "Many planets have more beautiful snow," he said.

"There are better snows on Lylo," Don said. "And better shadows, too. There are three moons there."

Bettyann knew they were giving her time to let the information settle into her mind. But it insisted on floating free, unmoored.

"This planet is famous for its greens," Robin said, more to himself than to Bettyann or Don. "There are some really startling greens in the tropical foliage, particularly Guam, for instance. But not here, not at this season, only this snow . . ."

"These are not your people," Don said from the alien body.

Bettyann looked at him again. The form began already to lose some of its compelling strangeness. She was coming to accept it. And now familiarly her emotions went out to it, and she longed to assure herself of its reality and the reality of her own true body beneath the Earth flesh.

"Let me help you," Don said.

Trembling, Bettyann began to change. She reached back along unfamiliar paths toward the new compartment of her mind. Utter complexity there: a twisted skein of controls. Again unrealized patterns swirled her thoughts; and like birds southward in winter, the thoughts knew direction from instinct. It was slow and painful at first, and she bit her lip to keep from crying out. And then, as she felt her body move upon itself, she was stunned by the miracle, wonderful beyond belief, that vibrated on the edge of existence. Her thoughts were too overcome for understanding: there was only a sense of awe, of humbleness, that here, within herself, she bore the great secret that could unlock the matter of her body and change it and release it and fashion it and mold it. She knew the new shape; she knew its lines; she knew its outward form: it was there in the compartment; and the compartment was not a second mind, not a greater mind at all, but something distinct from that, something apart from her personality, and wonderfully, wonderfully subservient to her thoughts. The transformation continued, with increasing speed, with increasing ease. And yet, she had never seen before; could hardly believe now, and they had shown her. It was too . . . alien.

It will take time, she thought, for the strangeness to leave. At first, so strange, and then, so new, and then (time is a wonderful thing) so natural after all. (And Dave had said, "If you walk over a path long enough, they'll pave it.")

"No," she said, her mind still quivering with the shock of the change and with the new (but not yet certain) freedom of her new form. "No," she said dully. There was the sense of belongingness: the absolute certainty of it, beyond everything, beyond feelings, thoughts: she belonged; it was right. "No," she said again. "They are not my people." She looked down to see how awkwardly her earth clothing draped on the alien body, and she tugged at the dress, and, for a moment, she felt sad and isolated.

"Then you will come with us?"

She started to say, "Yes. Yes, I will go. I must go, mustn't I? You are my people." But all the impressions, all the jumbled-together memories out of the past, rose within her, moaning. She tried to squeeze them away, tried to forget the now re-experienced excitement she had felt but two weeks ago at knowing she stood upon the brink of discovery (even now, still stood: still on the brink). My people are from the stars, she thought, unbelieving. And they go where they will, free and unbound. (And I told Doris I'd give her my history notes tomorrow, and I had an idea for an *Outlook* article.) She waited for her emotions to quiet.

"Give me a minute," she said. Emotions bubbled, frightfully out of control, and moved upward in her like furious hot water toward the top of a pan. (She stood feeling the strange body and watching Robin at the window staring into the snowfall.)

She had, once, a nightmare that her room was gone; above the stairs, at home, was nothingness; and when she awakened, moonlight fell on the carpet, and there were Momma Jane's soft hands, hands that had been there, quieting, as long as she could remember and before she could remember. And downstairs there were lacy curtains and nine (she had counted them often) twelve-inch albums of music that Dave, sometimes, after supper, listened to, and some day she would put the music into a painting, along with how Dave felt and how she felt (and there was a new compartment in her mind that would help her mold paints to her will and show her many things to be done and to be shown). And there was once a family of mockingbirds nesting in the withered oak tree; in summer, they sang all night, and through the open windows she could listen until sleep came. She could taste the night summer air (with sweet hyacinth and mystic lily of the valley and polleny honeysuckle and spicy rose). And it was neither happy nor sad, the memory that came, wrapping up everything in a flash of the five senses colored by time, but strangely wonderful, and she remembered with quiet amazement until her blood tingled.

Don shuffled restlessly.

Watching the stars, ever so far away, sometime before she entered school—very early, one of her first memories which merged into warm, assuring, nonmemories of the impalpable before. . . . They were hard and bright and intensely inviting, and she wanted to gather them like flowers. (Wasn't there a children's story about a little girl who wanted the moon, and one day she was gone, and her Daddy, pointing, said: "She's up there, she rowed away on a moonbeam," and the townspeople all shook their heads because it was sad?)

(Old man Starke was dying of cancer.)

But looking at Robin, old/young Robin, so very wise, she felt vast longing, longing more than earth longing, and the stars were spread out in a thousand excitements at her fingertips, and the wonder of it, vast, eternally vast, overcame her. (A blazing sun to play with, and spin beyond, and a dead sun to make you ask never-to-be-answered questions; and a thousand planets, and blue water, and sound and movement, and love of space; and never understanding, until a comet comes from nowhere, and it makes you know, and know, forget, and try to remember again . . . later . . . in a quiet time.) She wanted to fall down on her knees before the thought and throw out her no longer arms in a gesture of gratitude for these, her people, and she wanted to cry: These are my people, and this strange body is my body, and these are the ones who will understand me because they are what I am.

These are my people, and the sad-funny people and the world I have known, merely . . . human. . . . These, my people, and her blood raced with excitement, and she said, "Yes. Yes. I'll go. You are my people."

The words were said. And now she wanted to cry.

Robin was at her side. She looked up, and her heart raced with hope. "I've got to tell my parents good-bye first," she said. "I've got to tell them. I couldn't leave without telling them."

"I am sorry," Robin said after a moment. "I think I can imagine how you must feel. But that is impossible. To permit that would be to risk exposure. We ask only to be let alone; in return we let others alone. We waited for you here when your parents . . . seemed to want to question us. We did not want any trouble."

"But I just can't leave! I've got to see them again! I've got to tell them I'm going away!"

"The others will be waiting now," Don said. "We have delayed departure for you. We cannot wait any longer."

"You must write your good-bye," Robin said.

"Please . . ." she said.

Robin shook his head. "It is the rule, Bettyann. It has always been the rule. If this race were to discover our visits, if your parents found out. . . . No, the risk is too great. I cannot answer to the others. We ask only to be let alone; that is not too much to ask."

Slowly she changed back to the form of a college girl with a withered left arm, withered because it was more comfortable than the whole one which she would scarcely know how to use. (And she wondered idly with part of her mind, what would Bill say to see me with two arms, and where is Bill now—in the army somewhere—and does his handsome face, or the meaning of it, the memory of it, the . . . does it really matter what he would say or think? I could let the arm grow, a little at a time, a fraction of an inch a day, and get used to it, and tell everyone that some kind of exercise was making it grow again, and in a year when it was whole they would not think it strange, nor I. And I'm being a child to cry.)

"I'd . . . I'd like to be alone," she said. "I'll be all right after a bit. Please leave me alone for a few minutes."

"There is a pen and stationery on the desk," Don said.

When they came back, Robin said, "Do you feel better now?"

And she said, ". . . yes . . . I have written a letter to the college telling them that I have been called home by illness. They will not contact my parents and worry them about my absence." She looked at Don. "I wrote my parents a letter telling them I must go away." She looked at Robin, appealing for understanding. "It wasn't easy to write."

Robin said, "I am very sorry, believe me. But perhaps a letter will be best for you. I'll give them to the man at the desk downstairs."

Don said, "We'd better go."

"We have a car outside," Robin explained. "We have a scout ship several hours away."

They left the room, and, in the lobby, Robin roused the sleepy clerk and said, giving him the two letters and a bill, "Will you mail these first thing in the morning?"

(And Bettyann thought: It will take three days, maybe four days, for Jane to get it, and she will take it from the mailbox . . . and she will stand by the mailbox, perhaps open the letter before going back inside—if it isn't too cold on the porch that day. Open it by tearing neatly the right-hand edge, and shake out—or perhaps reach inside with thumb and forefinger after—the single page and the large-scrawled and few, pathetically few, words.)

They were in the car, and they drove through the cold night, and Bettyann trembled, sitting between Robin (driving) and Don, until finally noticing, Robin said, "Better turn on the heater, Don."

Robin drove slowly, and the night was long. Don dozed fitfully beside the window. At first Bettyann knew rising excitement that she could scarcely contain—not unmixed with sorrow but stronger. After a while she turned to Robin to ask him to hurry, and then, suddenly desperate, she wanted to talk to overcome the sickness of parting, but she could not find the words. Finally, her mind grew weary, and she wanted to sleep and forget (or perhaps dream a moment of flashing stars).

Night was endless. And then false dawn, gray and angry with snow clouds. And then the faint pink of real dawn, making her mouth feel dry and her head feel heavy.

Don roused, and after a while he consulted a map. "Turn right. The next road."

Slowly the world around them—flowing past them—awakened. They skirted a town.

". . . there's an odd red," Don said. "On that boy's cap, Robin."

Bettyann stared eagerly through the window. The boy, pumping his bicycle, his breath steam, sailed a newspaper away in an arching curve to a porch, and Bettyann remembered how it was to hear the thump of a morning paper against the side of the house, when you were still half asleep, and it was winter outside.

Suddenly fully awake, Don said, "They don't see much, do they? Were you able to show them anything?"

". . . a little," Bettyann said.

"Their eyes are different from ours, I think. It must have been difficult," Don said.

Still looking out the window, she wanted to explain something of how she felt. "Old man Starke sold his hardware store and put all his affairs in order because the doctor told him he had cancer and was going to die before summer."

Don smiled, distantly. "You can tell us very much about the natives. Believe me, I'm sure we shall all enjoy listening to your experiences."

There was not indifference in his voice; indifference was too easy a word for it. It was as if he were agreeing politely to something he did not quite understand; or as if he thought a great fuss were being made over a trifle. But he did not know old man Starke, did not know that old man Starke kept candy suckers behind the counter to give to children when their parents made purchases. (To be sure, it was good business: but there was more than good business in his smile, and the candy was something more than good business, too: it was more complex than good business.) And she could remember the smile and the voice (where was the cancer? in the throat?) saying, "My, how she's grown, Mr. Seldon, and I think I have just the thing for her sweet tooth today." (Always as if this generosity were not his usual practice, but something highly special just for you.) And on that occasion, he waved the not-yet-wrapped paintbrush (Daddy Dave bought it to paint the sink drainboard with, and then reconsidering called in Mr. Olson to do the job instead), and the hardware store smell of oil and new iron, or how new iron *should* smell. But that was something Don could not know. And never having experienced, might not feel as she felt . . .

"Turn here," Don said. "We go straight ahead."

The houses began to fall away to be replaced by fields. The rocky ground seemed to protest cultivation. Everything was dead, and rich dirt showed through rifts in the snow. The air was crisp, and the sun was hard and bright.

The car purred on. A railway line circled in to parallel the road, and a train puffed at the grade. The train fell behind the car, and after a bit, Bettyann heard it whistle sadly for a crossing.

"Tell me about the planets," Bettyann said. "Tell me what I'm going to see."

"There's so much . . ."

"I'd like to paint. What can I paint?"

"Paint? Well, there's Oliki. It's a really beautiful blue lake."

"I'd like to paint something like that field there, I think," Bettyann said.

"But isn't it a bit colorless, don't you think?" Don said, and there was honest surprise in his voice, as if it had never occurred to him to paint a field.

"I guess you've seen so many things. . . . Yes, I guess it is. But don't you see how, in spite of all the rocks and the snow, how everything is all huddled up, waiting to come alive?"

Robin said helpfully, "Yes, that's a fact, all right."

And Don said, "Left, here."

They drove for several miles in silence. They came to a rambling, high-sided bridge over an icebound creek (the ice above the center current was no thicker than scum). The boards of the bridge rattled under the weight of the car. Once across it, Robin swung the car onto a fisherman's path. The path was closely pressed by dead tree branches which clawed at the metal roof with brittle fingers.

"We won't need the car any more," Don said. "We can leave it here."

Robin jolted the car to a halt, and the three of them got out, and Robin said, "You were right, Don. No one's come by. It was a safe place."

The ship rested thirty or forty yards into the forest. There was a dead, charred area around it.

"Well, can you change now, all right, Bettyann?" Robin said.

"I think I can," Bettyann said. She let her form waver and change, and now it was easier, and suddenly compelled to exact their approval, she felt of the power in the compartment and began to work with it.

"A little tree!" Don cried happily. "A little tree, Robin! Look how pretty the leaves are! She's a very good tree!"

(The air was chill. The sun, bright through hazy clouds.)

"She learns quickly," Robin said.

She changed again, this time not into anything that she knew, but as her feelings guided her.

Don stared deep into the grayness that had been, a moment before, a tiny tree in bright, full foliage, and then he turned away shuddering. "That isn't very pretty, whatever it is," he said.

She let her body relax into her real form, the form into which she belonged, and for a single instant, she seemed too tightly held and oddly uncomfortable, and earth words came difficultly from her new mouth, and she could not yet think to them, for she knew no language, and she realized that, on the long drive, they had been thinking in conversation beyond her. She said, "It was . . . sadness, I guess you'd say. How I feel about leaving."

"We'd better get in the ship now," Robin said.

And Don helped her up.

When they were in the air, looking down at the trees falling away and backward, Don said, "You must be very excited. You have a great deal to look forward to."

But her emotions, in the moment of severance, were too great to permit an answer. She stood quiet and the window fogged with low clouds. Already the forest was lost in swirling grayness. And the ship increased speed. She was caught and held by the cold metal walls, and she wanted to pound them futilely with her fists. Home was far away below, far away, and farther even as she thought, and farther still, and dwindling, dwindling, beyond her grasp.

"The Big Ship is not far off the coast of Mexico," Robin said. "We will be there soon."

Bettyann wanted to hold on to something, for she was sick with movement. It will pass, she told herself, it will pass. She thought of the stars, and of the body, her body, and the alien lips moved, and she thought: These are my people.

The ship rose. It turned slowly toward the west. And time passed, little or great, and the clouds lay behind them, the Great Lakes below, like fingers curled up from behind the horizon.

Then, after a while, new fields and new forests, new streams and wide plains (and a huge river gashing the red earth). And after that, shooting high, the young mountains with toothy sharp crags biting at storm clouds that were teasing their summits. And snow sparkled on the peaks.

The ship quivered with flight and sang good-bye to the land far below. (And now the West Coast below, which she saw for the first time, would never see again, and dawn was upon it.

"Tell me about the planets," she pleaded. "Tell me quickly."

"You'll be able to see for yourself shortly," Don said.

"But tell me a little. Right now. Please."

"Well, there are the orange mountains of Kenu."

"What are they like?" she asked intently, trying to hold all of her attention together on his words.

"You'd just have to see them. We usually spend a whole day there."

"A . . . day?"

"That's not too long for the orange mountains," Don said.

"No," Bettyann said. "I meant how could you really see everything in a day?"

"I don't quite understand," Don said.

"I should like to *know* the orange mountains. Are there any streams there?"

". . . I can't say about that. Are there, Robin?"

Robin, at the controls, cleared his throat. "I can't say that I've ever noticed."

"But the colors, don't you see, Bettyann," Don said. "The texture of the colors."

"That's right," Robin said. "The colors. That's the important thing . . ."

Below lay the ocean, a tortured wash of deep green and gray: and white foam bounced like mad-dog slaver. The water changed to crystal sparkles and blue, deep blue, lighter blue, and then blue that was flat and waiting. A tiny steamer threw morning smoke. And night lay just ahead, for the ship outpaced the sun.

"There's always a great deal to see," Don said suddenly. "There are many sights," and Bettyann walked toward the rear of the ship.

Don thought to Robin, "She is a strange one."

Robin peered down, and moonlight was upon the water. "There's the Big Ship," he said. He dipped the scout toward it. Ocean roared up. He steadied the scout under his hands.

"The landing port's open, I see," Don remarked.

Bettyann looked down at the silver ship below. It lay upon the waves and rolled gently with them, and the landing port gaped like a hungry mouth, and the ship was a sleek, waiting prison.

If she were home now, she could tell Dave and Jane she had gotten sick at Smith and that she'd borrowed the money from June and hurried home because she was afraid to be sick among strangers. And then, after the letter came, after she had destroyed it, she could say she was well again and go back to Smith. She'd miss a week or so, but they'd let her back in after saying what a silly goose she'd been for not reporting to the dispensary instead of carrying a stomachache, that *might* have been appendicitis, halfway across the continent. It would be easy to pretend to be sick because she knew of her body now and she could counterfeit any symptom.

And then she realized the wonderful thing she bore within herself. So far, in the few hours of knowledge, she had only scratched the surface. What secrets were there? How much did she know that doctors never suspected? That artists never imagined? That . . . She thought of old man Starke, and what was the strange, rampant growth inside *his* body?

Did she know?

She became vastly excited at the thought of what it might mean to uncover the secret of herself. And now, for the first time, dimly but with overpowering certainty, she looked forward toward tomorrow knowing what her job would be and what her role was, and she was trembling.

But it was too late.

Below lay ocean in all directions, cutting her off from escape, and she looked at Don and Robin and felt a great sadness for them and for herself, and in all directions, bridgeless, the ocean rolled away to far horizons.

And Robin settled the scout inside the mother ship and berthed it.

Don walked back to her. "Do not cry," he said. "We are here." He smiled. "Let's get out. We're in the Big Ship. You're really home. Ready to travel at last."

"We are?" she said.

They climbed out into the huge hangar.

"I'll check the chart room before I close the port," Robin said. "There may be another scout out."

Don bent to inspect a pitted place in the hull of the scout.

After a moment, Robin came back. "No. They're all in. I'll close the port."

"I'll tell Bettyann. She'll want to watch the takeoff from the chart room."

Robin's feet pounded away. The port clanged shut. The feet came back. "What's wrong?"

"That's funny. She was here a moment ago. Bettyann! Oh, Bettyann! . . . I can't seem to find her . . . Bettyann!"

"I know she'll want to watch the takeoff," Robin said.

"Bettyann!" Don called, his voice echoing away unanswered.

Puzzled, they looked at each other and shook their heads.

"Bettyann!" Don called, and, "Where the devil is she?" Robin said.

And outside the mother ship the moon was low and the sea rolled lazily like an exhausted lover and the stars were far away in jet. Above the gentle sea, a lone, great bird flapped its powerful wings against the night.